**When a deadly traitor threatens
to dishonor a top-secret agency,
A YEAR OF LOVING DANGEROUSLY
begins....**

Marcus Waters
Long, lean, with mesmerizing blue eyes

*He'd been sent to exotic Cascadilla Island to keep
an eye out for Simon, the menacing mystery man
SPEAR seemed on the brink of capturing. Finding
a beautiful stranger on a sea-swept beach wasn't
part of his plans. But he made her his first priority
when he learned she was the victim of a
kidnapping....*

Jessica Burke
A strawberry-blond beauty with big brown eyes

*Jessica didn't know who her kidnappers were; she
only knew that she'd never felt so safe as she did
in the strong arms of Marcus Waters. So much so
that she gave him her innocence in the heat of the
night....*

"Simon"
Still nameless, still faceless—and still
just as deadly

*He was on his way to Cascadilla, not knowing
what lay in wait for him. Could this trip to the
Caribbean be Simon's undoing?*

Dear Reader,

Valentine's Day is here this month, and what better way to celebrate the spirit of romance than with six fabulous novels from Silhouette Intimate Moments? Kathleen Creighton's *The Awakening of Dr. Brown* is one of those emotional tours de force that will stay in your mind and your heart long after you've turned the last page. With talent like this, it's no wonder Kathleen has won so many awards for her writing. Join Ethan Brown and Joanna Dunn on their journey into the heart. You'll be glad you did.

A YEAR OF LOVING DANGEROUSLY continues with *Someone To Watch Over Her*, a suspenseful and sensuous Caribbean adventure by Margaret Watson. Award winner Marie Ferrarella adds another installment to her CHILDFINDERS, INC. miniseries with *A Hero in Her Eyes*, a real page-turner of a romance. Meet the second of bestselling author Ruth Langan's THE SULLIVAN SISTERS in *Loving Lizbeth*—and look forward to third sister Celeste's appearance next month. Reader favorite Rebecca Daniels is finally back with *Rain Dance*, a gripping amnesia story. And finally, check out *Renegade Father* by RaeAnne Thayne, the stirring tale of an irresistible Native American hero and a lady rancher.

All six of this month's books are guaranteed to keep you turning pages long into the night, so don't miss a single one. And be sure to come back next month for more of the best and most exciting romantic reading around—right here in Silhouette Intimate Moments.

Enjoy!

Leslie J. Wainger
Executive Senior Editor

Please address questions and book requests to:
Silhouette Reader Service
U.S.: 3010 Walden Ave., P.O. Box 1325, Buffalo, NY 14269
Canadian: P.O. Box 609, Fort Erie, Ont. L2A 5X3

Margaret Watson

Someone To
Watch Over Her

Silhouette®

INTIMATE MOMENTS™

Published by Silhouette Books

America's Publisher of Contemporary Romance

Special thanks and acknowledgment are given to
Margaret Watson for her contribution to the
A YEAR OF LOVING DANGEROUSLY series.

For Dad. Thank you for all you've done for us.
But most of all, thanks for always being there for me.

 SILHOUETTE BOOKS

ISBN 0-373-27128-X

SOMEONE TO WATCH OVER HER

Visit Silhouette at www.eHarlequin.com

Printed in U.S.A.

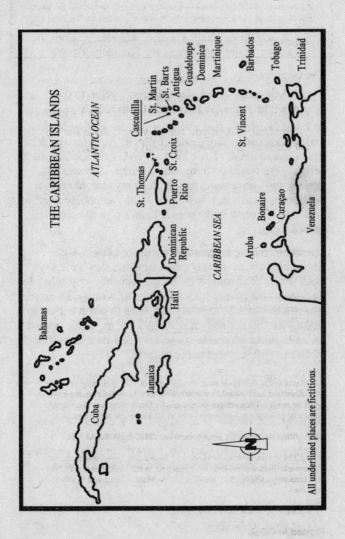

THE CARIBBEAN ISLANDS

ATLANTIC OCEAN

Bahamas

Cuba

Jamaica

Haiti

Dominican
Republic

St. Thomas

Puerto
Rico

St. Croix

Cascadilla

St. Martin

St. Barts

Antigua

Guadeloupe

Dominica

Martinique

Barbados

Tobago

Trinidad

St. Vincent

CARIBBEAN SEA

Aruba

Bonaire

Curaçao

Venezuela

N

All underlined places are fictitious.

A note from talented writer Margaret Watson,
author of over ten novels for Silhouette Books:

Dear Reader,

I hope you are enjoying Intimate Moments' fabulous
A YEAR OF LOVING DANGEROUSLY series as much
as I am! I certainly had a wonderful time writing Marcus
and Jessica's story. *Someone To Watch Over Her* and all
the books in the A YEAR OF LOVING DANGEROUSLY
series bring you everything that Intimate Moments is
famous for—adventure, danger, mystery and, of course,
passionate romance. I'm waiting just as anxiously as all of
you for each book in the series. I can't wait to read every
one of them!

I've been reading Intimate Moments books since the
line started almost twenty years ago, and they've always
been my favorite romances. That's probably why, when I
decided to pursue my lifelong dream of writing, I wanted
to write Intimate Moments. I still have to pinch myself to
make sure I'm not dreaming when I see my name printed
on an Intimate Moments cover, my book on the shelf next
to all of my favorite romance authors.

Writing romances is a big change from my other
profession. I'm also a veterinarian, which is why you'll
find an animal or two in almost all of my books. A lot
of people ask me how I could give up a wonderful career
as a veterinarian to write books. My answer is that
veterinary medicine is my job, but writing is my passion.
And being a romantic through and through, I always
follow my heart.

Sincerely yours,

Margaret Watson

Chapter 1

Marcus Waters kicked at a shell on the sand and watched it somersault into the frothy blue waters of the Caribbean. It reminded him of his heart, he thought sourly, tumbled and tossed by his futile passion for Margarita Alfonsa de las Fuentes.

Shoving his hands into his pockets as the shell disappeared into the sea, Marcus continued walking down the deserted beach. It was just as well, he told himself, that Margarita had chosen Carlos Caballero. He wasn't interested in a long-term relationship. Hell, he wasn't interested in any kind of a relationship, except for the ones that ended with a goodbye kiss in the morning.

Sure, he'd been half in love with Margarita. But then, who wouldn't have been? The sexy SPEAR agent was beautiful and bright and had stirred his hormones since the first time he'd met her, years ago, when they had both been starting out with the covert

agency. Working with her again had reignited the
spark that had lain dormant for so many years.

It was better this way, Marcus told himself as he
rounded another curve on the long, lonely beach.
Margarita and Carlos belonged together. And he belonged by himself. He'd learned that years ago when
he'd chosen his career with SPEAR rather than a
woman he'd loved.

He pulled the loneliness around him like a cloak,
using it to harden his heart and seal it against any
more painful blows. He had his job, and that was all
that mattered. That was all he wanted.

And right now, his job was to spend time on this
beautiful tropical island, waiting for the elusive
Simon to show up. Once he did, Marcus would keep
an eye on him and report back to the agency so they
could close in on him. Simon had been attacking the
SPEAR agency for several months, trying to destroy
what had taken over a century to build. The Stealth,
Perseverance, Endeavor, Attack and Rescue agency
had been started by Abraham Lincoln during the Civil
War, and had been handling the government's most
dangerous and covert problems ever since.

Marcus was just one of a dozen agents dedicated
to catching Simon and stopping his ruthless campaign. And their intelligence had told them that
Simon was headed here to Cascadilla. But until
Simon arrived, Marcus would employ his cover as a
tourist on vacation and enjoy all the pleasures this
idyllic island had to offer.

As he walked slowly down the beach, avoiding the
shells and sea glass, he noticed the gulls and other
shorebirds screeching and diving toward a dark bundle on the sand. Wondering if it was something that

had washed off a boat, he walked a little faster. After years as an agent, he paid attention to everything. His life could depend on knowing the details.

There were pale tentacles on the bundle, and he frowned as he walked a little faster. The hairs on the back of his neck stood up, and suddenly he broke into a run. That was no bundle of seaweed. That was a body, lying half in the water and half on the sand.

The gulls wheeled off, shrieking, when he dropped to his knees next to the body, which was facedown in the sand. It was a woman. Her wet reddish-blond hair was tangled and matted with sand and salt. Marcus reached for her neck and felt a pulse, thready but present. Reassured that she was alive, he ran his hands over her quickly, looking for broken bones. Finding nothing, he gently turned her onto her back.

Several small cuts and bruises on her face were dark red against the bright pink of recent sunburn, but the skin beneath the collar of her T-shirt was pasty white. He watched the rise and fall of her chest for a moment, reassured that it was regular and even, then put his ear against her ribs and listened to her breathe. Her lungs were clear, which meant that she hadn't almost drowned.

Marcus rocked on his heels and stared at the unknown woman. She looked very young, and although she was bedraggled and bruised, he could see that she was beautiful.

What had happened to her? How had she ended up on this deserted part of the beach, unconscious and alone?

Once again the hairs stood up on the back of his neck. His instincts were working overtime. Quickly he glanced up and down the beach, but he didn't see another soul. And he hadn't passed anyone on his walk. He wondered if she had swum to the beach, then lost consciousness.

He couldn't leave her lying in the sand. He scooped her into his arms, grunting as he stood up. His left arm was still tender from the bullet he'd taken in Madrileño. But he forced himself to ignore the pain as he headed back to his beachfront cottage at the Westwind Falls Resort.

Her body felt chilled in his arms, and in order to keep her warm he shifted her so that most of her body pressed against his. The weight of her breasts flattened against his chest, and her nipples burned into his skin through the thin, wet material of her shirt. Her thigh brushed against his groin, electrifying him.

His hands tightened on her firm, smooth skin, and instinctively he pulled her closer. His body stirred, shifting and adjusting to touch more of her.

Shocked at his unexpected response, he adjusted her in his arms so that she wasn't pressed so intimately against him. But she groaned softly and moved restlessly against him, and once again they were touching as intimately as lovers.

"Hell, Waters, get a grip," he muttered. He clenched his jaw and walked a little faster. "The woman's been injured, for God's sake."

The lights of the resort twinkled through the gathering darkness, and he exhaled with relief. The sooner he got this woman to his cottage and called an ambulance, the happier he would be. His reaction to her closeness was unsettling and disturbing.

He shifted her again, holding her more firmly, and began to jog. His arm throbbed, but he ignored the pain. He knew his cottage was close. It stood slightly apart from the others, the last in the row before the development surrendered to the beach and the dense tropical foliage that began at the edge of the sand. Since Westwood Falls Resort was owned by SPEAR, this cottage was always available for an agent who needed it.

He hadn't bothered to lock his door, and he used his hip to push it open. He walked through the comfortable living area, then laid the woman in his arms gently on the bed in the large bedroom. Then he took a step back and looked at her as he absently massaged his arm.

Her eyes were still closed, and her mouth had a bluish tint. But her chest was rising and falling regularly, and when he lifted her eyelids and looked into her eyes, her pupils were equal in size and reacted to the light.

She looked small and fragile and vulnerable lying on the huge bed. Once again he realized that she was very young, probably in her early twenties. "What happened to you?" he asked, assessing her. "How did you end up on that beach?"

That would be up to the police to find out, he told himself. She needed to get to a hospital. He picked up the phone that stood on the nightstand next to the bed and began to dial the local emergency number. But before he finished dialing, the woman cried out.

"No!" The single word reverberated with panic. "No, don't."

Quickly he set the telephone receiver into its cradle and knelt next to the bed. "It's all right," he said in a low voice. "No one's going to hurt you."

Her eyes remained closed, but her hands clenched

into fists on the bedspread. "Stay away from me! Get out!"

He reached for her hand and cupped her tight fist between his palms. Her hands were small and delicate, the bones tiny and fragile. "Relax," he murmured. "You're safe now."

Her hand gradually released its fist, then she turned her palm to his and gripped him tightly. "No!" she yelled again. Her hand jerked away from him and swung wildly in the air. "Why are you doing this?"

What had happened to her? He stood up slowly, his gut churning with anxiety as he stared at her. Whatever had happened to this woman was more than an accident. Someone had deliberately tried to hurt her. And judging from where and how he had found her, she was probably still in danger.

Warning bells clamored in his head. His gaze lingered on the restless woman on the bed, and he made a split-second decision. He wasn't going to call the police until he'd had a chance to talk to her. He had to make sure that he wasn't putting her in danger all over again by alerting the authorities to her presence. For the time being, she would be safe with him.

She cried out again, and he sat on the bed with her. "You're safe now," he said, taking her hand again. "I'm going to keep you here until you wake up and can tell me what happened to you. Do you understand?"

He spoke in a low, soothing voice. She couldn't hear him, but perhaps that primitive place deep in the brain that judged danger would hear and understand that she was safe. He continued to talk to her, his voice quiet and gentle, until she stopped moving around on the bed. When she was quiet again, he let go of her hand and stood up.

"You can't just let her lie there in those wet clothes," he muttered to himself. "And you have to examine her thoroughly. If you're not going to call an ambulance, you're going to have to take care of her yourself."

Her simple T-shirt and shorts were beginning to dry, and they were stiff with sand and salt. The sport sandals still on her feet were covered with sand and grit. He took those off first, then brushed the sand from her feet.

He unbuttoned the waistband of her shorts and slid the zipper down. But when his hands brushed over her skin at her waist, a sizzle of electricity shot up his arm, and he froze in place, unable to move.

Her skin was as soft as a butterfly's wing and as smooth as cream. His hands were suddenly burning hot against the coolness of her skin, and he clenched his fingers around the waistband of her shorts to stop himself from touching her.

Appalled, he pulled his hands away as if he'd been burned and jumped up. He stared at the unconscious woman, feeling the heat of need rush through him. What the hell was the matter with him?

Shaken, he picked up the phone again to call for an ambulance, but hesitated before he'd punched in the numbers. This woman was in danger, he reminded himself. And he had sworn to protect those in danger. It was part of his code of honor, both professionally and personally. It wasn't her fault that he couldn't control himself.

Just because he was acting like a randy teenager didn't mean he had to throw her to the wolves. He swallowed once and sat on the bed. He could do this. He could think of her as an impersonal object that needed his help.

His resolve lasted just long enough to remove her shorts. Tossing them on the floor, he looked at the tiny scrap of lace that she wore beneath the shorts and swore long and hard. A blond triangle of hair was visible beneath the almost-transparent lace. And although he estimated she was only a few inches taller than five feet, her legs seemed to go on forever. Slim and firm, they were evidence that his mystery woman led an active life.

Scowling, he deliberately looked away from her legs and grabbed the hem of her T-shirt. This was ridiculous. The woman was unconscious. He was the only person who could help her right now, and that's what he would do. He could tame his hormones into submission.

But when he pulled the T-shirt over her head and tossed it on the floor, he closed his eyes and groaned. The bra she wore matched the lacy panties and did about as much to hide her body. He forced his gaze to her face and told himself his job was about her health and safety and nothing else.

"Snap out of it, Waters," he growled to himself. "This woman already has enough problems. She doesn't need you making a fool of yourself."

Steeling himself, knowing he had to check her from head to toe, he forced himself to think of all the things that could be wrong with her. Then he began to examine her, utilizing the basic medical training that was part of every SPEAR agent's education. He tried to ignore how she felt, ignore the softness of her skin and the smoothness of her body. He could block her beauty out of his mind, but it was more difficult to ignore the way her vulnerability touched a soft spot he didn't even realize he still had.

Finally he stood up and draped a blanket over her. His hands were shaking and his mouth was dry. It was best to pretend that she didn't have any effect on him, he told himself.

"You don't seem to be too badly hurt," he said to her, even though she was still unconscious. With an effort of will, he forced himself to ignore his physical reaction to her. "If you can hear me, you need to know that you're safe now. You've got a bunch of scrapes and bruises, especially on your legs, but nothing is broken. And since there are no cuts, bruises or bumps to your head, it doesn't look like you have a head injury, although we'll have to wait until you're awake to know for sure. You're going to be plenty sore when you wake up, but I think that's about all."

Certain that he'd made the right decision about calling for help, he walked into the bathroom and started the water running in the bathtub. Then he walked out and crouched next to her again. "I'm going to give you a bath. You're covered with sand and salt, and I don't want it to irritate your skin."

He stopped, reaching for the control that had never failed him before. She was a stranger who needed his help, he reminded himself. But he swallowed once before he continued. "I know this is pretty personal, but you'll thank me for it in the morning."

Would she? Or would she be horribly embarrassed that someone had undressed her and bathed her while she was unconscious? "Let's get that underwear off of you. It's not doing much good, anyway," he muttered.

Steeling himself, he quickly peeled away the tiny scraps of lace and chiffon that passed for underwear. He tossed them on the floor, then slid his arms around her, trying not to notice how perfectly she fit against him, and carried her into the bathroom. He placed her gently in the tub, where he quickly sponged off the worst of the grit.

"You'll have to do the rest yourself after you wake up," he muttered after a few minutes. The sight of her perfect breasts and lithe young body had made him as hard as granite. "I know it's not your fault, but I can't do this anymore."

He grabbed a towel from the rack and wrapped it around her, then carried her to the bed. Peeling back the bedspread, he laid her on the sheets, leaving the towel wrapped around her.

"I can't leave that on you." He scowled. The large bath towel covered her body, but it was damp and she would be shivering in a few minutes. He rummaged in a drawer and pulled out one of his T-shirts. "This should work."

He eased the towel away from her and quickly pulled the T-shirt over her head. It floated down her body, covering her almost to her knees. He breathed a sigh of relief, which turned into a scowl when he realized that it did nothing to hide the curve of her breasts and the outline of her nipples. His hands ached to weigh her breasts, to feel their weight in his hands, and he jerked the sheet over her body. "I'll be in the other room."

Night had fallen completely, and the sky was dark velvet over the black of the Caribbean. Stars glittered in the sky, reflected in the water like sharp diamonds. The muted sound of voices and the low laughter of women drifted on the breeze from the common areas of the resort.

Marcus ignored the sounds of merriment that wafted from the resort. He stared into the darkness, looking down the beach, probing the foliage near his cabin. Who was out there? Where were they hiding? What predators prowled the night?

Somewhere, someone was looking for the woman who lay on his bed. Someone who meant her harm. The familiar adrenaline of a case rose inside him, making his heart pound, sharpening his senses. No one would hurt her, he vowed. He would make sure of that.

He picked up his cellular telephone and dialed a number he had memorized. After two rings a voice said, "Devane here."

"This is Waters," Marcus said. "Have you heard anything about a missing woman?"

"No." Marcus could hear the interest sharpen in Russell Devane's voice. "What do you have?"

"I'm not sure. I found a woman washed up on the beach about a half mile from the resort. There wasn't anyone else around, and she didn't have any identification. She's still unconscious."

"What are you going to do?"

"Wait until she wakes up, then find out what's going on. I hoped you or one of the others might have heard something."

"Not a word. But we'll keep our ears open."

"Let me know if you hear anything."

Marcus closed the phone and went into the bedroom to look at the woman once more. She hadn't moved from the place he'd set her down. But he could see that she was shivering.

Gently he drew the bedspread over her, then reached for the extra blanket. "No one knows a thing about you," he murmured. "Devane would have heard if there was anything to hear. Who are you, mystery woman? And how did you end up on that beach?"

His only answer was the steady rise and fall of her chest. "I'll be in the other room if you wake up," he said. He let his gaze linger on her for another moment, then he turned and walked out of the room. It would be wise not to spend too much time with her, he told himself. The effect she had on him was too intense and too disturbing.

It would be better once she woke up. He was sure the attraction would disappear once she was conscious and talking to him. What could he have in common with such a young woman?

He felt much better as he sat on the sofa. That was the answer, of course. Once she was awake, he would see that she was just another woman, beautiful but very young. Once she was awake, this ridiculous state of arousal would quickly disappear. Hell, he wasn't interested in relationships, anyway. Hadn't they just established that he was better off without Margarita or any other woman? Hadn't he learned his lesson all those years ago when Heather had forced him to choose between her and his career with SPEAR? His mystery woman would tell him what had happened to her, he would help her deal with it, and they would go their separate ways. It was that simple.

Marcus grabbed the book he had started reading earlier, but put it down after only ten minutes. Restlessly he stood and paced around the living room. Finally, unable to stop himself, he stepped into the dimly lit bedroom. The woman on the bed was still unconscious, but she had moved. She lay on her side and looked as if she was sleeping. Her left hand was tucked under her cheek, and her right hand was curled under her chin. He'd apparently managed to get most of the sand out of her hair, because it was drying in a soft golden cloud around her face. She looked innocent and helpless, and another fierce wave of protectiveness flooded through him.

He might not know much about relationships, but he knew how to protect a woman. And that's what he would do. He'd get her back safely where she belonged and make sure that nothing else happened to her.

He adjusted the blanket around her shoulders, then crouched next to the bed again. "You're going to be all right," he said in a low, comforting voice. "You're safe now, and you're not badly hurt. Sleep for as long as you like. When you wake up, we'll figure out how to help you."

She moaned in her sleep, but it didn't sound as frantic and fearful as her earlier cries. Her forehead wrinkled as if she was trying to figure something out. Then she was quiet and still again.

"It won't be long before you're awake," Marcus said, familiar enough with injuries to know when someone was regaining consciousness. "I'll be close by when you do."

He stood, intending to walk to the living room. But he was oddly reluctant to leave her alone. She would be frightened when she woke up. She wouldn't know where she was. Maybe he should stay with her.

"She'll think you're one of the people who hurt

her, you idiot," he growled to himself. "Get out of here."

He moved into the other room, but couldn't sit down to read. He paced the small room, then went and stood on the tiny porch.

The sounds of the tourists' voices were lower, muted and more intimate. It was the end of the evening, and soon everyone would be returning to their cottages and rooms. The time for shared gaiety and laughter had passed. Now couples would be dancing more slowly, their bodies touching, hands twining together. Men and women would exchange heated glances, allow their hands to linger just a little longer. Soon everyone would steal away and the resort would be silent and still.

Marcus scowled and walked inside, closing the door firmly behind him. He had a job to do, and the woman on his bed had become part of his job. He'd damn well better remember that.

He threw himself onto the couch and picked up his book again. After staring at the same page for too long, he closed the book and leaned back, willing himself to get some rest.

He had just fallen into a restless sleep when he heard a noise from the bedroom. It sounded as if someone was walking around. He leaped to his feet and ran into the other room.

The woman was no longer lying on the bed. She was standing next to it, swaying, gripping the chest of drawers for support.

Panic leaped into her eyes when she saw him. She grabbed a nail file that had been on the dresser. "Stay away," she said, her voice low and husky. "I have a weapon."

Chapter 2

Jessica Burke gripped the chest of drawers with one hand and held the pitifully small nail file tightly in the other. Fear and anger throbbed inside her, and she welcomed it. Her head ached and her legs wobbled, but she wasn't about to give an inch to the man who stood in the doorway.

He hadn't been one of the two men who had grabbed her in her workshop, but that didn't mean a thing. He was probably the one who'd ordered her kidnapping, the Simon that her two kidnappers had talked about.

"I'm not going to hurt you," he said, his voice deep and quiet. He stood and watched her, making no effort to come any closer.

"You expect me to believe you?" Jessica tried to put as much scorn as possible in her voice.

To her shock, the man smiled at her, and Jessica felt her stomach swoop toward her toes. She scowled and gripped the nail file more tightly. She must have gotten a blow on the head, she told herself. How else could she explain her reaction to a man who had kidnapped her?

The man's smile disappeared. "You have no reason to trust me," he said, his voice still quiet, "but I mean you no harm. My name is Marcus Waters and I found you on the beach just before dusk this evening. You looked as if you'd been washed ashore."

Jessica studied the man in front of her. Rangy and tall, at least a head taller than her own petite five feet four inches, he looked like any other tourist in the Caribbean islands. His blond hair was a little too long. He was dressed casually, in shorts and a T-shirt, and he had sandals on his feet. But his blue eyes burned into her with the intensity of a laser. Those were not the eyes of a casual tourist.

"Are you taking me to Simon?" she demanded.

His face tightened for a moment, and she saw a flare of shock in his eyes. Then it was gone and his face looked no different than it had a moment ago. But there was a new wariness in his eyes.

"Who's Simon?"

"I was hoping you could tell me that."

He shook his head slowly. "I told you, my name is Marcus Waters. I have no idea who Simon is."

"You're lying." He'd reacted to the name, she was certain of it.

He watched her for a moment, then he nodded toward the bed. "Why don't you sit down? I promise not to come any farther into the room. But I'm afraid you're going to fall."

Jessica damned her rubbery legs and spinning head, but she knew he was right. If she didn't sit down, she would fall. And she would lose any advantage she had over him. Gingerly she moved to the bed and perched on the edge, realizing she wore nothing but an unfamiliar T-shirt. Her lack of clothing, and the knowledge that this stranger had undressed her, made her feel even more vulnerable.

"Where am I?" she demanded.

"You're on Cascadilla," he said promptly. "At the Westwind Falls Resort. This is one of their beachfront cottages." He paused, then asked, "Do you know where Cascadilla is?"

"Of course," she began, then stopped abruptly. Until she knew more about this man, she wasn't going to answer any of his questions. "I know where Cascadilla is. But how do I know you're telling me the truth?"

Marcus nodded at the telephone. "Pick it up and dial zero," he said. "The front desk will answer."

Without taking her eyes off him, she reached for the phone and fumbled it out of its cradle. She punched in zero, then held it to her ear. When the operator said, "Westwind Falls Resort, front desk, how may I help you?" she hung up the phone.

"All right, so you're telling the truth about that. That doesn't mean I trust you about anything else. Even a criminal can stay at the Westwind Falls."

"But he would have to be a very wealthy criminal," he said smoothly. "Since you know about the Westwind Falls Resort, can I assume that you live on Cascadilla?"

She clamped her lips together. "I'm not going to tell you anything. In fact, I'm not going to stay here. I'm going to walk out the door, and you'd better not try and stop me."

"Or you'll stab me with the nail file?" His eyes softened, and she saw a glint of admiration in them. "I'm not trying to keep you here against your will. You're welcome to go. But before you do, maybe you ought to think about how you got here. Who hurt you? And are they still out there, waiting for you?"

Jessica bit her lip as the fear crashed over her again. For the past few minutes, as she was sparring with the man in the doorway, she had forgotten her ordeal. Her eyes slid to the telephone again. "Maybe I'll just call the police."

"Go ahead, if that would make you feel better. But how do you know they're not involved?" His eyes took on a cynical glint. "Money can buy just about anything in the islands."

She knew that far better than most. And he was right. "Then I'll call my family."

"Why don't you let me help you?" he said softly. "At least tell me your name and what happened to you." He paused, and his eyes hardened. "And how this man Simon is involved."

"Why are you concerned?" she retorted. "Why would you want to help me? And what do you know about Simon?"

He shrugged. "I'm in law enforcement. And I'm the one who found you. I'm curious about what happened to you."

"You recognized the name Simon," she said, watching him carefully.

She saw the jolt of surprise in his eyes and felt a fierce satisfaction. Then his face was carefully blank again.

"I've heard the name," he finally said. "Someone

here at the resort must have been talking about a man named Simon. But I have no idea who he is.''

Could she trust him? She couldn't trust anyone, she told herself. But he *had* offered to let her call the police. If he had wanted to hurt her or turn her over to the man named Simon, he'd had plenty of opportunities while she was unconscious. And she needed to know what had happened in those lost hours since she'd jumped off the boat and woken up in this room.

''Why don't you first tell me how you found me, and where?'' she said.

He nodded. ''That's only fair.'' He hesitated. ''Do you mind if I come in the room and sit down? This may take a while.''

Jessica shook her head slowly. ''No.'' She watched while he settled his long frame in a chair on the other side of the bed and realized he'd done it deliberately so he wasn't blocking her escape route. She allowed herself to relax just a little.

He leaned forward, fixing her with his gaze, and a hum of electricity seemed to fill the room and shiver along her nerves. He let his hands dangle between his knees, and she found herself staring at them. What would it feel like if Marcus Waters touched her? When she realized what she was doing, she sat upright with a start. What was the matter with her? What was she thinking? She didn't even know this man.

When she let her gaze meet his, she was startled at the intensity in his eyes. They bored into her, making her shiver.

''I was walking down the beach,'' he began abruptly, holding her gaze but banking the intensity in his eyes. ''It was close to dusk and there was no one else around. I saw what I thought was a clump of seaweed on the beach, then I realized it was a body." He paused and waited, as if gauging her reaction.

"Go ahead," she said.

"It was you. You were unconscious, and it looked as if you'd been washed ashore. I made sure you didn't have any broken bones and checked to see if you had any head injuries. When I couldn't find any, I picked you up and carried you back to my cottage."

"Did you call the police?" she demanded.

He stared at her for a moment, measuring her, then shook his head. "I had the phone in my hand, but then you cried out. It was obvious you were frightened of someone, that someone had hurt you. So I decided to wait until you woke up before I called anyone. I wanted to talk to you first."

Jessica narrowed her eyes as she stared at him. "It seems odd that you wouldn't call the police. Isn't that the obvious thing to do?"

Marcus stood and moved to the window. He opened the shutters just enough to look outside. While he was staring into the darkness, he said, "I told you, I'm in law enforcement. I had a bad feeling about what happened to you. I wasn't sure if calling the local police was the smart thing to do. That's why I wanted to wait until you woke up."

Slowly he turned to face her. "Do you want to call the police now? Are you sure they can keep you safe? Or would you rather tell me what happened and let me help you figure out what to do?"

God help her, but she wanted to believe him. Appalled, she stared at the man standing across the room from her. What was the matter with her? This man was a total stranger, and she wanted to trust him with her life.

She was a scientist. She needed proof, concrete evidence. She needed facts. But a reckless part of her that had been deeply buried had somehow reappeared. She wanted to believe him without proof. She wanted to tell him what had happened to her. She wanted to believe that he could help her, that he was on her side.

She was drawn to Marcus Waters, and the realization scared her. She was intelligent enough to know that she was reacting to him the way a woman reacts to a man. She didn't know anything about men, about dealing with them as a woman. Her dating life was practically nonexistent. But she yearned to trust this man in front of her.

She hesitated for a moment, her analytical side struggling to control her emotional need to connect with Marcus. Finally she nodded. "I'll tell you what happened."

"Thank you." He moved to the chair, sat and leaned forward, his arms resting on his legs. "What's your name?"

She hesitated again. This was the first test. Taking a deep breath, she said, "My name is Jessica Burke."

"All right, Jessica, what happened to you?"

He didn't recognize her name, she realized, and relief flooded through her. He didn't know who she was or who her parents were. Surely that meant he wasn't involved.

You don't know this man, she reminded herself. *He could merely be a good actor.*

But she'd managed to read him easily enough earlier, when she'd been quite certain he was trying to hide his reaction to the name Simon. She had to trust her instincts. They were all she had right now.

"I'm a scientist," she began slowly. She saw the flicker of surprise in his eyes and ignored it. "My parents live on a private island not too far from Cascadilla. I have an office near my parents' home that I use when I visit them. My office is a small building near the beach, somewhat isolated and quite a walk away from the main house."

"You work there by yourself? That doesn't sound very secure." His voice was neutral.

"It hasn't been a problem before now," she replied.

His eyes gleamed, but he nodded. "Go ahead."

"I was working this morning, close to noon, when the door opened. I didn't pay any attention because I thought someone from the house was bringing me lunch. When I finally looked up, there were two men in front of me. I knew right away that I was in trouble. I screamed, but I'm sure no one could hear me. They threw a blanket over my head and wrapped it around me, then picked me up and carried me out the door."

He leaned forward. "Doesn't your father have a security system?"

"He does, but one of the men apparently had worked for my father. He bragged to the other man that he knew how the security system worked and was able to get around it."

"Then what happened?"

"I bit one of them. Badly. It was through the blanket, but I'm sure I drew blood. He cursed and swore and dropped me. I was able to run a few steps, but then the other one caught me again."

"Good for you." Jessica saw approval shining in Marcus's eyes and felt ridiculously happy.

"It didn't do much good in the end. They still threw me into their boat and sped away. It was all over in a few minutes. And no one in my parents' house had any idea that I was gone."

"Then what happened?" He leaned farther forward. "Did they hook up with this man Simon?"

"No. I heard them talking about him. The man I bit was named Steve, and he seemed to be in charge. Tommy was the man who worked for my father, and Steve told him that Simon wouldn't be happy if they let me get away."

"Do you know Simon? Is he someone your parents know?"

"I have no idea who he is. I know my parents don't know anyone named Simon."

"You sure you've never heard the name before?"

"Mr. Waters, those two men were kidnapping me. Don't you think I would have remembered if I'd ever heard the name Simon before?" she said tartly.

Slowly he leaned back in his chair. "Did you figure out what Steve and Tommy were going to do with you?"

"I assumed they were delivering me to this Simon, but I didn't stick around to find out."

Once again admiration gleamed in his eyes. "How did you get away?"

"They didn't bother to tie me up. I guess they figured there wasn't anywhere for me to go. I managed to get the blanket untangled enough to see where we were headed, and once we got close to Cascadilla, I recognized it. I guessed that was where we were going, and I knew I couldn't let them get me wherever they intended to take me.''

She hesitated, unsure how much to reveal. Finally she said, ''I've always heard that you have to do anything you can during a crime to prevent being taken somewhere else.'' She didn't tell him that her father's security force had drummed that into her since she was small. ''So I knew I had to get out of the boat. When we were close enough that I thought I could swim to shore, I wriggled out of the blanket and slipped over the side of the boat. Steve and Tommy were too busy trying to navigate to notice that I was gone. Then I just dove under the water and stayed there for as long as I could. By the time I surfaced, the boat had almost disappeared over the horizon.''

''How far away from the beach were you?'' Marcus asked.

She shrugged. ''Maybe a mile.''

His eyebrows rose. ''You were able to swim a mile to shore?''

''I'm a strong swimmer. It's part of my job.'' Her mouth twisted. ''And I was desperate. It's amazing what you can do when your life depends on it.''

Marcus's mouth softened, then he stood up and came around to her side of the bed. He sat down inches away from her and took her hand. ''You're a brave woman, Jessica Burke.''

His hand was warm and strong around hers, and it sent an unexpected wave of sensation jolting up her arm. She held on to his hand and stared at him, and she watched his eyes darken. She might be naive, but she had no trouble identifying the expression she saw in his eyes. It was naked desire.

A curl of answering desire unfurled inside her, and

she stared at him with shock. This wasn't supposed to be happening. She didn't know Marcus Waters, she reminded herself. And you were supposed to know someone well before you had sexual feelings for him. That's what all the books said.

She slid her hand away from his, ignoring the shimmer of regret. For a moment he leaned forward, his eyes fixed on hers, and she wondered with a thrill if he would touch her again. She saw the intent in his eyes. Then he leaned away from her, carefully shuttering his gaze.

"So you swam to shore after you jumped off the boat. What happened then?"

"I have no idea."

His eyebrows came together in a frown. "What do you mean?"

"I mean I don't remember much of what happened after I jumped off the boat. I remember swimming for a long time, but the details are fuzzy. I must have passed out once I made it to shore."

"Did the guys in the boat, Tommy and Steve, notice you were gone?"

"I'm sure they did, eventually," she said dryly. "But I don't think they knew right away. They didn't come after me with the boat, if that's what you're asking. I don't remember seeing it." She shrugged. "But then, I don't remember much."

"Did you hit your head at some point?" he asked, his voice sharp.

"I don't think so." She touched her head tentatively. "It doesn't feel like it."

Marcus stared at her, an assessing look in his eyes. "So why did Steve and Tommy want to kidnap you? What do you have that they want?"

"I have no idea."

"You said you're a scientist. What do you do? Could your work somehow be involved?"

"I doubt it. I study coral reefs. And although I find the subject extremely interesting, I doubt anyone would kidnap me because they had a burning need to know about coral reefs."

His mouth curled in a tiny smile. "Not only beautiful, but humble, too," he said in a voice layered with velvet.

Once again she felt the jolt of attraction. This time it shimmered through her whole body, pooling low in her abdomen until she felt like a violin string quivering with tension.

"Just realistic," she managed to say.

The smile lingered in his eyes as he continued to stare at her. Then slowly the smile faded. "That leaves the other possibility. Money. Would you or your parents be able to pay a ransom?"

She nodded tightly. It was something her father and mother had feared for years. "Yes. My parents would be able to pay a ransom."

"Even a sizable one?"

"Yes." Her voice was curt.

"I'm not going to ask them for one," he said. "I'm just trying to establish a motive here." He leaned back and watched her. "So you don't know anyone named Simon, but your parents could pay a ransom. That must mean that they have a lot of money." He paused. "Have there ever been kidnap attempts before? On you or anyone else in your family?"

"Yes." She looked away. "Someone tried to kidnap my brother years ago."

"Did they succeed?"

"No. He managed to get away. But since then, my father has had very elaborate security for both of us."

"Yet someone managed to get through it and grab you."

"I told you, one of the kidnappers had worked for my father and had managed to figure out how to get around the security." She hesitated. "And there isn't as much security on the island. My family are the only people who live there. We've always felt safe on the island."

Marcus nodded, his eyes unreadable. "Then we have to assume that you were kidnapped for a ransom. Is that what you think?"

"Yes. It's the only thing that makes any sense."

"Do your parents have enemies who might try to hurt them by kidnapping you?"

"Anything is possible, I suppose," she said slowly, weighing the possibility. "But I can't think of anyone." She looked at Marcus. "A wealthy man always has enemies. But I don't know of any that would do this."

"Do you have any enemies of your own?"

"No." The very idea was ludicrous. "I've lived a very sheltered life, Mr. Waters. All I've done is go to school and study."

"My name is Marcus," he said, his low voice strumming across her nerves. "And it looks like you have some enemies now."

"Yes, it does."

She was caught in his gaze, held like a deer in the headlights of a car. She couldn't get away, and she wasn't sure that she wanted to. Her heart stuttered in her chest and sped up, and butterflies danced in her stomach.

What was happening? She had never felt like this around a man before. The realization that she was attracted to Marcus Waters both thrilled and frightened her. She had no experience with men, let alone a virile, sexy man like Marcus. She had no idea what to do.

To change the subject, she plucked at the T-shirt she wore. "What happened to my clothes?"

"They were covered with sand and salt. They would have irritated your skin, so I took them off and gave you a bath."

She swallowed, her skin burning beneath the thin shirt. "You gave me a bath?"

"I couldn't let you stay in those clothes."

She was uncomfortable, knowing that he had seen her naked. Heat flared in his eyes as he watched her, and she knew that he was thinking about the same thing. A flush started at her feet and swept up her body.

"I'm sorry," he murmured, but she could see that he wasn't sorry at all. And suddenly, shockingly, she wasn't sorry, either. Blood pounded in her head, and desire swept through her veins. "Don't be," she whispered. "It's all right."

What was wrong with her? She shuddered, then buried her face in her hands. It must be the shock of what had happened. She had never felt like this before, never ached for a man to kiss her. For God's sake, he had seen her naked, and rather than being upset, she was thrilled at the thought!

"It's all right," Marcus murmured, and he wrapped his arms around her. "You're safe now."

His tenderness, and the comfort she drew from his embrace, opened up a hidden place in her heart. "I hated being so helpless," she said fiercely. "I've never been helpless in my life."

She could feel him smile into her hair. "Somehow that doesn't surprise me," he said.

She raised her head to look at him. "You've probably never felt that way. I'm sure you're always in control."

The smile faded from his face. "You're wrong," he said quietly. "That's how I know how you feel. You're only in control when you can't be hurt. And I was hurt once, a long time ago, by someone I loved. I felt just as helpless as you do now. And that's one of the reasons I didn't call the police. I wanted you to know that you were in control again."

"That's very thoughtful of you."

For a moment she saw need and vulnerability deep in his eyes. Then they hardened. "Don't get the wrong idea. I'm not a thoughtful person, Jessica."

But he was. She had seen the careful way he'd moved around her, trying not to alarm her. She'd noticed how he always left her an escape route. From the moment she'd woken up, he'd tried to set her at ease.

She shuddered, remembering her fear, and he wrapped his arms around her. He held her gently, but her skin burned where he touched her. Her stomach lurched and her heart jolted in her chest. Instinctively she stiffened against him, but he smoothed his hand down her back and held her more closely.

"You're shivering again. It's all right, Jessica. It's just the adrenaline. No one can hurt you now."

He thinks you're upset about being kidnapped. She told herself to push away from him, to tell him the truth. She was upset about the way she was reacting to him, a total stranger.

But he wasn't a stranger any longer. He had rescued her and taken care of her. He was willing to help her. No, Marcus Waters wasn't a total stranger.

And even though she told herself to move away from him, she leaned into his embrace. He stroked her hair and murmured in her ear, and she quivered in his arms. He was trying to comfort her, and she was becoming aroused.

He would be appalled if he knew, she thought. But just as she told herself to move away, to put some distance between them, she felt the tension in his arms, heard the thundering of his heart against his chest. Was it possible that he was feeling what she felt?

She raised her head to look at him and was stunned at what she saw in his face. Need, naked and raw, glittered in his eyes. For her. She drew in a sharp breath, unable to look away.

The look in his eyes changed to one of fierce possession. He held her gaze for a moment, then bent his head to hers.

Chapter 3

The first brush of his mouth was tentative. She could feel him holding back, hesitant. And she knew that the smart thing to do was lean away from him, murmur thanks for all he'd done, then slip quietly away from Marcus Waters.

But a part of her she didn't recognize, a wild, untamed part that had lain dormant for all of her twenty-one years, pushed aside the rational voice in her head. Instead, Jessica curled her arms around his neck and pressed against him.

He felt solid and tough, his chest and legs hard and unyielding against her softness. It felt as if his heat would consume her until there was nothing left of her but the aching at her core. She felt helpless in his arms, completely overwhelmed. But she trusted him, she realized. She had connected to Marcus on some level, and she didn't want to move away. Instead of frightening her, his heat and desire thrilled her, increasing the throbbing deep inside her. She twisted against him, not sure what she wanted but knowing that she wanted more.

He groaned and crushed her lips beneath his, devouring her mouth. When she gasped with surprise, he plunged into her mouth, tasting and caressing her with his tongue.

She tightened her arms around him, and he groaned again. Pulling her closer, he pressed her more tightly against him until every part of her was touching the hot, hard length of his body. Pressure coiled deep inside her until she squirmed against him, searching for something she couldn't name.

"Jessica," he groaned, tearing his mouth away from hers. "Tell me to stop."

"I don't want you to stop," she whispered. She wanted to be joined to him, to know everything possible about Marcus Waters.

He swept his hand down her back, lingering at her hip, shaping the curve of her buttocks. She could feel his hand tremble against her. "I want you," he muttered. "I don't want to stop, either."

"Then don't," she said recklessly, throwing all caution to the winds. She was lucky to be alive tonight. And suddenly she wanted to know what she had been missing all those years she'd spent in the lab doing nothing but working and studying. Knowing she might have been killed, she wanted to know what it felt like to be fully alive.

He pulled back a little, and she felt him staring at her. She opened her eyes with an effort. The desire that glittered in his blue eyes made her feel drunk with power. She had done that, she thought. She had made this man want her. And holding his gaze, she reached up and kissed him.

He kissed her with his eyes open, watching her, seeing her response to him. And as he kissed her, as his hands roamed over her back, she saw his eyes darken, felt his muscles harden even more. He reached up and brushed the hair out of her eyes, and she realized he was trembling.

Suddenly he picked her up and laid her on the bed. "You're so beautiful," he murmured as he leaned above her. He traced the curve of her cheek to her neck, and his hand lingered at the top of the T-shirt. "I didn't bathe you very well, you know."

"Why not?"

He stared at her, his eyes hot and dark. "Just looking at you made me hard. By the time I put you in this bed, all I wanted to do was touch you."

Jessica swallowed. "You can touch me now," she said, her voice husky and low. She hardly recognized herself. This wasn't Jessica Burke, the woman whose middle name was cautious, who had never had a serious relationship.

The neck of the T-shirt gaped between her breasts, and he let his fingers linger there, sending fire shooting through her veins. "Are you sure, Jessica? It's not too late to say no."

"I don't want to say no." A part of her was appalled, but her body throbbed wherever his fingers slid over her. And the ache inside her was too urgent, too all-consuming to be denied.

He watched her for a moment, then bent his head and pressed his mouth to her collarbone, his hand still between her breasts. His lips and tongue tasted her, teased her, until her hips moved restlessly beneath him.

When he lifted his head his eyes gleamed. "You taste wonderful. But I'll bet there are other parts of you that taste even better."

Slowly he pulled the neck of the T-shirt down until her breasts were exposed. She jerked when she felt the cool air brush across them and instinctively reached to cover herself.

He stared at her hand for a moment, then looked at her again. His eyes were almost black, and tension vibrated out of him. He held her gaze as he bent and kissed her, and she felt all her muscles go slack.

"Move your hand," he whispered. "Wouldn't you rather have me touching you?"

Her hand fell to the bed beside her, and he kissed her again. Then he raised his head to look at her. She felt her nipples getting hard just from his gaze.

He propped himself on one elbow, and his hot gaze swept her body. Then he lightly traced the curve of her breast with one finger. When she shivered, he cupped her with one hand. "They're just as beautiful as the rest of you," he whispered.

The throbbing was almost unbearable. She felt like Marcus was slowly winding a spring tighter and tighter inside her. When she twisted toward him, he closed his eyes briefly, then opened them to stare at her. He drew one finger across her nipple.

The jolt stunned her, and she cried out. She watched his face tighten, then he touched her again. She couldn't stop the moan that started deep in her throat.

Suddenly he bent and took her nipple in his mouth. She bucked against him, overwhelmed by the sensations. Her body felt completely foreign to her. Nothing mattered except the touch of Marcus's hands and the feel of his mouth. A sharp need throbbed deep inside her, and she instinctively moved her legs apart.

Marcus slid his hand to her thigh, and his fingers traced circular patterns on her skin. A whirling vortex pressed down on top of her, drawing her inside it. When Marcus slid his hand up her thigh and lingered between her legs, she rose to meet him. The sensations crashing over her were almost unbearable.

Marcus grabbed her shirt with an urgent hand and pulled it over her head. She was naked in front of him, but she didn't care. She had gone too far into the vortex to think about modesty. Instead, she reached for him, trying to unbutton his shorts.

"Let me," he whispered. "If you touch me now, it will all be over much too soon."

He stripped off his T-shirt and tossed it to the floor, and she stared at his chest. Dark blond hair swirled around his nipples, and she ached to touch it. Then he pulled off his shorts, and her eyes widened.

He watched her look at him while he reached into a drawer of the night table and pulled out a foil packet, which he opened quickly. Then he kissed her again, his hand sweeping over her body, sending hot licks of fire down every nerve.

"Shall I show you the other places that taste good?" he murmured.

She was incapable of speaking. Her tongue was thick in her mouth, and her head was spinning. He stared at her for a moment, then let his mouth trail between her breasts and down her abdomen. She jumped when he bit the inside of her thigh.

Then he put his mouth between her legs, and she

cried out with shock. His tongue caressed her slowly until she knew she would go out of her mind. Tension coiled inside her, tighter and tighter as he gently suckled her.

The world exploded around her. Spasm after spasm shook her body, and all she could do was cling to Marcus. She felt the hard length of him probing her, and she lifted herself to meet him.

She felt herself stretching and stretching, then suddenly he stopped. When she opened her eyes, he was staring at her.

"You're a virgin." His voice and his eyes were full of shock.

"What difference does that make?" she asked, her voice wobbly.

"It makes a hell of a lot of difference," he retorted. He tried to move away from her, but she wrapped her arms around him and held on tightly.

"Please don't stop."

She felt him quivering in her arms, felt the tension that pulsed from him. "Are you sure?"

"Yes. Please, I want you to make love to me."

He groaned and pressed his forehead to hers. "You're a virgin, Jessica. It's going to hurt."

"Only the first time, right?"

He stared at her for a long time, and she could see that he wanted to stop. He was trying to move away from her. So she wrapped her arms around him and pulled him to her. He took her mouth in a deep kiss and pushed into her with one stroke. Then he lay still.

The pain was sharp and stinging, but after a moment it receded. Then he began moving slowly and gently. At first it felt like she was being stretched beyond the limit, but as her body began adjusting to him, she felt sensation stirring all over again.

Wrapping her arms around him, she held him close as the tension built. Then suddenly, she exploded all over again. Marcus tightened his arms around her and shuddered above her, whispering her name.

They lay tangled together, unmoving, for a long time. When the world finally stopped spinning, she shifted her hands so that she could explore his broad, solid back.

He moved to his side and propped himself on one elbow as he stared at her. There was a shadow of sadness in his eyes.

"You should have told me before I touched you," he said.

"I wanted you to touch me. I wanted you to make love to me."

"How could you know what you wanted, when you'd never done it before?" He reached over to brush the hair out of her face, a gesture that seemed almost unconscious. "I took something that I had no right to take, Jessica."

"You didn't take it. I gave it to you." Her voice was fierce.

The sadness seemed to fill his face. "Your virginity should have been a gift to the man you love."

"I didn't feel like waiting around for him," she said tartly. She reached up and touched his face. "I wanted to make love with you, Marcus. I'm old enough to make my own decisions."

"Just how old are you, Jessica?"

"I'm twenty-one, almost twenty-two."

"And I'm a very old thirty-five." He stared at her for a moment, then he lay down and pulled her close.

"God help me, I know I shouldn't have done that. But I can't regret it if you don't."

"Not for a minute," she said. She turned so that she was cuddled against him. "Stay with me, Marcus," she said, and she heard the weariness in her voice. She was already half-asleep.

"I'm not going anywhere."

Marcus looked at the woman wrapped around him and cursed himself long and silently. He was a real bastard. He should have stopped the moment he realized she was a virgin. Hell, he told himself, he shouldn't have started in the first place.

He'd known she was upset, known that she needed to be comforted. But what had started out as an innocent embrace had become anything but innocent. And it had happened very quickly.

He'd been too aroused, too hot for her, to be able to think rationally. And she hadn't done anything to stop him.

It wasn't up to her to do the stopping, he reminded himself. Once he realized she was a virgin, that had been his responsibility.

She murmured in her sleep and moved closer to him, and he tightened his arm around her. She was only twenty-one years old, for God's sake. She was far too young for him.

But he had never responded to any woman the way he'd responded to Jessica. The heat of their lovemaking still lingered, and he was becoming aroused all over again just thinking about it.

It was the circumstances, he told himself. That would explain this intense, uncontrollable attraction. It was a well-known fact that danger and excitement were potent aphrodisiacs. Satisfied with his explanation, he closed his eyes and allowed himself to pull Jessica closer against him.

The hushed stillness of the deepest part of the night surrounded him when he woke suddenly. He could feel that Jessica was awake, too. She was tense and silent beside him.

"What's wrong?" he whispered.

She turned to him, and he saw the fear fading from her eyes. "I'm all right now," she whispered. "I woke up and didn't recognize the room, then I remembered being kidnapped. It just took me a moment to figure out where I was."

"You're safe, Jessica."

"I know." She stared at him in the darkness, a pale sliver of moonlight falling on her face from the window, and he wanted her all over again. She must have seen the need in his face, because she reached up and put her arms around his neck. "Kiss me, Marcus."

He knew he should untangle himself and tell her to go back to sleep, but he couldn't look away. Desire raged inside him, and her dark eyes were luminous with need. Slowly he bent his head until he was kissing her, and as her mouth opened beneath his, he felt a rush of need fill him.

She must have felt the same thing, because she turned so she lay pressed against him from her chest to her toes. Almost as if they had a will of their own, his arms came around her and pulled her tightly against him.

He gave in to the need coursing through him and covered her body with his. This time, he tried to be gentle and careful, as he should have the first time. This time, he tried to go slowly. But she arched her back and cried out for him, urging him inside her, and he lost control.

And when she lay clasped around him, her fingers digging into his shoulders, her mouth fused to his, he poured himself into her, feeling the ripples of her release clamping around him. He drank in her cries and clasped their hands together, holding on to her tightly.

They fell asleep still bound together, holding hands. Marcus's last thought was that nothing had felt this right in a long time.

The sun was shining through the window when he woke up again. He stretched, then went still as he realized that he wasn't alone in the bed. He looked at Jessica's blond hair and knew that the night before hadn't been a dream. It had been very real.

He couldn't remember ever wanting another woman the way he had wanted Jessica. The way he still wanted her, he admitted. And he couldn't remember lovemaking ever being so powerful or moving him so deeply.

And how was he going to deal with that in the light of day?

He eased away from the sleeping Jessica and slid out of the bed. But instead of moving away, getting dressed, he stood staring at her. She was so beautiful in the morning light, and so young. A wisp of guilt fluttered through him. He had taken advantage of her. It was as simple as that.

He couldn't give her back her virginity, but he *could* protect her from whoever was trying to kidnap her. His jaw hardened. Not only was it his responsibility, it was part of his job. Simon was behind the kidnapping, he was sure of it. The traitor must be getting desperate for money if he was willing to take such a chance.

By keeping Jessica safe, he would force Simon out into the open. And further into the net. Yes, he would keep her with him until Simon was caught and all danger to her had passed.

He ignored the flare of pleasure at the prospect of having Jessica close by for an indefinite length of time. He was just doing his job. And his job was what mattered to him. No woman could compete with that.

He glanced at Jessica once more, then deliberately walked out of the room. He made coffee and put on some clothes, trying to put the magic of the night out of his head. He needed to concentrate on his job, but it was impossible to forget how Jessica had tasted and felt, how she'd responded in his arms.

Scowling, he walked into the bedroom with two cups of coffee, stopping in the doorway when he saw Jessica sitting up in the bed. She had pulled the sheet over her breasts as she leaned back against the headboard, and he felt himself getting hard all over again.

"Good morning," he finally said. What was he supposed to say to her? *I'm sorry I took your virginity last night and could we make love all over again?*

"Good morning." He saw a faint blush of pink on her cheeks and realized that this was a first for her, too. She'd never faced a lover after a night of passion.

Setting the coffee on the night table, he sat on the bed. Her cheeks became pinker. "About last night," he began, but she cut him off.

"Please don't apologize again. You'll make me feel very…inadequate." She plucked at the sheet and pulled it higher over her breasts. He could see the pink of her nipples through the light sheet, and he wanted to touch them again, feel them get hard and tight in his hand.

Then her words registered. "Inadequate?" He stared at her. "Believe me, Jessica, if I'm apologizing, it's not because you were inadequate." He took her hand and pressed it against his arousal, closing his eyes as need rocketed through him. "That's what you do just by looking at me."

He opened his eyes to see an answering need in hers. He dropped her hand and stood abruptly. "I brought you some coffee."

"Thank you."

She reached for the coffee cup, not meeting his eyes. And suddenly he understood. She didn't know the rules. Hell, she didn't even know how the game was played.

"Jessica, if I had stayed in bed with you this morning, we would have made love all over again. More than once. And I couldn't do that to you." He took her hand. "I don't want to hurt you. And I would have if we'd made love again." Pressing his lips to her palm, he said, "You're going to be stiff and sore this morning. I'm trying to be a gentleman here."

Finally she looked at him. "Thank you for explaining. I was afraid that..." She swallowed but continued to meet his eyes. "I was afraid that you were disappointed in me because I don't have any experience."

He groaned and pulled her against him. "Jessica, I can barely think of anything else when I'm near you. And neither of us can afford that right now. We need to concentrate on your problem."

"You're right. I should take a shower and get dressed."

He nodded. "Your clothes are dry, but they probably need to be washed. I'll give you some of my clothes to wear in the meantime." He looked at her again, at the faint outline of her curves beneath the sheet, then stood. "I'll get out of here so you can take a shower. I won't be responsible for my actions if I watch you get out of that bed."

Finally her face relaxed into a small smile. "I'll see you in a few minutes."

As he walked out of the room, he wanted to turn around and stay, wanted to step into the shower with her. But he forced himself to keep walking, to shut the bedroom door behind her.

He'd picked a hell of a time for his hormones to rage out of control. If his suspicions were correct and Simon had orchestrated Jessica's kidnapping, the SPEAR traitor must be very close. He might even be on Cascadilla already. Marcus couldn't afford to be distracted.

But he couldn't turn Jessica loose, either. He'd promised to protect her, and he always kept his promises. Marcus downed a gulp of scalding coffee and stared moodily out the window. He should never have touched her last night. Now that he knew what they were like together, it was going to be almost impossible to keep his mind on his work.

The bedroom door opened behind him, and he turned to see Jessica standing hesitantly in the doorway. Her hair was wet, and she wore another of his T-shirts and a pair of his cutoffs that hung to her knees. He'd deliberately picked a dark blue shirt for her to wear, but he could still see the points of her nipples pressing into the fabric.

He scowled at her, shoving his hands into his pockets to stop himself from reaching for her. "You look like something the cat dragged home."

She lifted her chin. "I thought you were the one who dragged me home."

He felt his mouth curving into a reluctant smile. "Touché. Come into the kitchen and have some breakfast. You must be hungry."

"I guess I am." She slid into a chair at the tiny table and looked at the fruit and muffins he'd set out. "I've almost forgotten when I had my last meal."

They ate in silence for a while, but it wasn't a comfortable silence. Memories of the night before danced between them. The silence grew louder and louder, and the tension stretched and swelled. Finally Marcus pushed away from the table.

"I'll throw your clothes into the washing machine." He was tormented by the sight of her wearing his clothes. Every time her shirt brushed against her breasts, desire clawed at him. Every time the neck of the shirt gaped wide, he had to stop himself from staring.

At that she looked quickly at him. "I can do that."

"Go ahead and finish eating. I wasn't very hungry," he said gruffly. He felt her gaze on his back as he hurried out of the room.

After he tossed her stiff, wrinkled clothing into the wash, he leaned against the machine for a few moments to compose himself. He could do this, he told himself. He could walk out there and have a normal conversation with her.

When he walked into the kitchen, she was standing at the sink, rinsing the dishes. Sunlight streamed through her blond hair, turning the red highlights to fire. Her legs were strong and tanned, and he noticed that she had painted her toenails a bright red.

"We need to figure out what to do next, Jessica," he said.

She carefully set a dish into the dishwasher, then turned to face him. "The first thing I need to do is call my parents. They must be frantic with worry."

He shook his head. "You can't tell anyone where you are."

Her eyes narrowed and she glared at him. "You may have rescued me, but that doesn't mean you own me. I'm going to call my parents, and you're not going to stop me."

Chapter 4

"It's too dangerous," he said.

"Why?" She flashed him a challenging look.

"Because we want the kidnappers to wonder what happened to you. We want them to worry about it. We want them to be forced into the open to ask questions."

"My parents wouldn't tell anyone where I was. And I can't bear to think about what they must be going through."

It would be best if she didn't make that call. But he could see the anguish in her eyes, her concern in the trembling around her mouth. Finally he picked up his cell phone off the counter. "You can use this," he said gruffly.

"Thank you."

"It has a scrambler on it so that no one can electronically eavesdrop." He scribbled Russell Devane's phone number on a piece of paper. "Tell them they have to act as if they haven't heard from you. They have to act as if you're still missing. And tell them if they get a phone call demanding a ransom to call this man and follow his instructions to the letter.''

She took the paper tentatively, as if she was afraid it might bite her. Then she looked at him, her eyes wide and troubled. ''Who are you?'' she whispered.

''Someone who wants to help you. And I have a few friends who can help, too.''

''You're no ordinary Good Samaritan,'' she said, measuring him with her eyes.

He saw the sharp flash of intelligence in her whiskey-brown gaze and nodded slowly. ''You're right. But that's all you need to know.''

She watched him for a moment, and he could see her turning what he'd said over in her mind. Finally she said, ''But I need to know who you really are.''

He hated to lie to her, but he had no choice.

''I told you last night that I was in law enforcement. That's the truth.''

Her eyes narrowed. ''You know an awful lot about medicine for a cop.''

He shrugged. ''I've had paramedic training. A lot of cops do, now.'' He would let her assume he was a police officer.

She tilted her head to one side as she examined him. ''I've never met a police officer like you before.''

''How many police officers do you know?''

''None,'' she admitted.

''That would make me your first.'' Need stirred inside him at his double entendre.

She blushed and looked away. ''I guess it would.''

He went to her and took her hand. ''Satisfied?''

She nodded slowly. "All right, Marcus, I'll do exactly what you say. And I'll tell my parents to call this number if anyone contacts them."

"Will they be able to maintain the facade of frantic parents?" he asked. "Will they be able to pretend they haven't heard from you?"

"I'm sure they will if I tell them my life may depend on it."

"Your life may very well depend on it," he said quietly. "Don't forget, your father already had one break in security. There may be other people working for him who are really working for this man Simon. You might remind your parents of that."

"I'm sure my father will interrogate everyone who works for him." Her voice was grim and her eyes cold. "If there's anyone there who doesn't belong, he'll find out."

Marcus shook his head. "You can't assume that. I know what you're thinking, Jessica. You're thinking that your father will make sure everyone on the island is trustworthy, then you can go home. But you can't go back to that island until your kidnappers have been caught."

He wasn't proud of the fact that his blood hummed through his veins at the prospect of spending more time with her. But it was true. He couldn't think of any other way to secure her safety than to keep her close by him.

Her gaze dropped, and he knew he'd been right on target. "I can't allow you to put yourself in danger for me," she said, her voice so low that he almost couldn't hear her.

"Why not?"

"Why not?" She raised startled eyes to his. "Because I can't take advantage of you that way."

"You're not taking advantage of me. I'm offering. I want you to stay." God help him, but he wanted her to stay with him more than he'd wanted anything in years. It was only because it was his best shot at catching Simon, he told himself. But he couldn't block out of his mind the images of the two of them making love.

"You must have a reason for being here on Cascadilla," she said. "I'm disrupting all of your plans."

"Not at all. I was here for a vacation. So you're not interrupting anything. Except maybe my sleep." Suddenly, overwhelmingly, he wanted her with a fierce need that he wasn't sure he could control. He held her gaze for a moment until he saw an answering heat pool in her eyes, then he looked away.

He moved to the other side of the room and shoved his hands into his pockets. "Go ahead and call your parents, but you won't be going home. Not until the kidnappers have been caught."

Her hand shook as she picked up the cell phone, but she didn't take her eyes off his face. "Are you sure?" she whispered.

Was he sure he wanted her to stay? "Absolutely." He'd never wanted anyone with this kind of mindless need, this kind of urgency. But that wasn't the reason he wanted her to stay. He tried to block out his personal feelings. She was part of his job, his only link to Simon. "I told you I would protect you, and I meant it. No one will hurt you again."

Her mouth trembled and softened as she watched him. Finally she murmured, "I believe you. You're a warrior, aren't you, Marcus? I'll be perfectly safe with you.''

He scowled. That depended on her definition of safe. "Yes. And you can tell your parents that you're safe. Just don't tell them anything else.''

"I won't.'' She took a deep breath and looked at the phone. Marcus waited until he heard her speaking, then he walked into the other room. She deserved at least a little privacy to talk to her parents. And he trusted her to do exactly as he'd told her. Jessica was intelligent enough to understand that her life might depend on it.

At least ten minutes passed before he no longer heard the murmur of her voice. Finally she came into the room. He could see that she'd been crying.

Without thinking, he rushed over to her. Holding her shoulders, he stared at her. "What's wrong? What happened?''

She shook her head and tried to smile. "Nothing,'' she said. "My parents were sick with worrying. They were so glad to hear my voice and know that I was okay.''

He loosened his grip on her shoulders but was reluctant to let her go. He told himself that she was upset and he needed to comfort her. Drawing her close, he wrapped his arms around her. When she leaned against his chest, he felt his heart lurch and begin to pound.

"Are you sure you're all right?''

She nodded against his chest, and he let his hand tangle in her hair. It trickled through his fingers like liquid silk, and he closed his eyes as her fragrance drifted up to him.

"It's been a rough twenty-four hours, hasn't it?" he said gruffly.

At that she lifted her head. "Some parts of it weren't completely awful," she said, and he saw the hesitation in her eyes.

"Some parts of it were wonderful. Last night makes me almost grateful to this man Simon," he said, his voice rough, and he bent to kiss her. She melted into him, and he cursed his insensitivity. Jessica wasn't a woman who knew the score. She had been a virgin, for God's sake. She couldn't know that what they had shared had been beyond wonderful.

Their lips clung together, and Marcus felt the now familiar surge of desire that overwhelmed him whenever he touched her. He groaned in the back of his throat as she moved innocently against him, and finally broke away from her.

"Tell me what your parents said," he said as he looked at her. He couldn't bear to let her go just yet, so he slid his hand down her arm and took her hand in his.

She looked at him uncertainly, then nodded. "You're right. We have to think about my predicament."

She had managed to read his mind, and it scared the hell out of him. He didn't want to feel this connection with any woman. After Heather, he had sworn he wouldn't give any woman the power to control him. To hide his reaction, he turned and sat on the couch, still holding her hand. She sat next to him, and he drew in a ragged breath.

"What did your parents say?"

"They were frantic with worry, of course. They didn't realize until close to dinner that I was missing.

As soon as they saw my office, they knew something was wrong. I guess I put up more of a struggle than I realized.''

"Why am I not surprised to hear that?" he murmured.

She shot him a sharp look. "What was that supposed to mean?"

He bent and pressed a quick kiss to her lips. It was all he would allow himself. "It means I almost feel sorry for the two guys who tried to grab you. I'm sure you fought like a hellcat." He gave her a crooked smile. "I know you already, Jessica."

"You're right," she said, staring at him for a moment then looking away. He was sure he saw confusion in her eyes. "I guess I did. There was a lot of damage in my office. When my parents couldn't find me on the island, they realized I must have been kidnapped. They've been up all night, waiting for a ransom call."

"They haven't gotten one yet?" He forced himself to concentrate on business. "No one's called and claimed they had you? Asked for a ransom?"

"No."

"They might, though," he said thoughtfully, his mind flying through the possibilities. "If you don't surface in a few days, the kidnappers might assume that you drowned while trying to swim to shore. I wouldn't be surprised if they called your parents anyway and tried to get ransom money from them."

"They wouldn't succeed," she said immediately. "My father wouldn't be taken in that easily."

"Parents will do a lot of things that seem irrational if they think their child is in danger," he said gently.

She started to shake her head, then paused.

"Maybe you're right," she said after a moment. "If I hadn't called them and let them know what had happened, they might be willing to grasp at any straw."

"Would your parents mind if someone put a tracer on their phone line? In case this Simon calls them?"

"I don't think so." She turned to face him. "But be prepared for questions. I told them you were some kind of law enforcement officer, but that wasn't good enough for my father. He wanted to know details. And if you go to the island to install that equipment, he's going to give you the third degree."

"No one would be going to the island. We couldn't risk it. I'm sure Simon is watching the island, and if he sees the activity, he'll know something is up. We'll have to do it from the other end. Someone will be in contact with the phone company."

"You seem to know an awful lot about this Simon."

He cursed his carelessness. That's what came from thinking with a part of his anatomy other than his brain. "I'm just using my experience as a cop to imagine what a smart kidnapper would do. And I think we have to assume that he's smart. After all, he found a way to get to you."

She leaned back against the couch and stared at him thoughtfully. "I wonder why this Simon decided to kidnap me."

That was a very good question. "Any ideas?"

She shook her head, but he could see her mind working. "I don't know," she said slowly. "I've been on the island for a while, but I've spent most of my time working. I come to Cascadilla very infrequently."

"All work and no play," he murmured.

She shot him a glance, then her mouth curled into a half-smile. "I can't say that anymore, can I?"

His pulse leaped, but she didn't seem to realize what her words did to him.

"I just don't get out very much," she continued.

He was going to get her killed or kidnapped again if he didn't get his head in the right place, he told himself savagely. Deliberately looking away from her, he struggled to control the desire that raged through him. Finally he said, "How long exactly have you been on your parent's island?"

"Since early in December."

He swung to face her. "That's a long time. Don't you have a job? Wasn't there someplace you needed to be? It's the end of January."

She smiled at him again, and it was like a punch to his heart. Her smile was open and unafraid, reflected in her eyes as well as her mouth, and it transformed her face. She had been lovely before, but now she was breathtaking.

Before he could recover, she said, "I'm working on a Ph.D., Marcus. I left school at Christmas break and now I'm working on my thesis. Since I didn't have any classes this semester, I thought I could work just as well at my parents' house, and be a lot more comfortable." She grinned at him. "And I don't have to cook for myself, either."

"So you've been living with your parents for almost two months." He leaned forward, staring at her. "Have your parents had any visitors?"

"They've had lots of visitors." She shrugged. "I've been too busy to pay much attention."

"Anyone you didn't know?"

"I didn't know most of them. A lot of the people who came to the island were my father's business associates." She shrugged again. "I did my work and came and went as I pleased."

"So he might have actually been on the island," he mused, almost to himself.

"You think Simon might have visited my father?" Her voice sharpened, and when he looked at her he saw fear in her eyes. "Are my parents in danger?"

So the fear was for her parents, not herself. He took her hand and squeezed it. Then, before he could stop himself, he brought it to his mouth and kissed her palm. "I don't think so," he said. Then he hesitated. "But we can't know for sure. Whoever this Simon is, he must be desperate to try to kidnap you the way he did."

"Do you think he'll go after my parents?"

Slowly he shook his head. "I doubt it. He still doesn't know what's happened to you. He's got to be hoping that you show up. And even if you don't, he might try and get some ransom money from your parents anyway."

"What about when nothing works?"

"Then I suspect he'll try something else. But your parents are probably safe. He'll know that they'll be wary and much more careful than usual. He'll choose an easier target."

"Like I said before, it sounds like you know Simon very well."

He knew far too much about the slippery criminal. He rubbed his left arm, feeling the fresh scar tissue beneath his shirt. But he had no intention of telling Jessica anything about himself. "I just know how criminals operate," he said easily. "It makes it easier to catch them if you know how they think."

She studied him, and the perception in her level gaze was disturbing. He didn't want to think anyone could read him easily. His life could depend on it. But Jessica Burke, whom he'd known for less than twenty-four hours, was watching him as if she could see all the way to the bottom of his soul.

She looked away, but he could feel the tension shimmering in the air between them. Jessica wasn't sure if she believed him or not.

Once again he marveled at her perception. And Jessica was only twenty-one years old.

That thought jerked him to reality. He had no business sitting here with this woman, who was barely more than a child, wondering when he could make love to her again. If the difference in age between them wasn't enough of a barrier, their difference in experience sure as hell should be.

Jumping up from the couch, he said, "I need another cup of coffee. Can I get you anything?"

Jessica watched Marcus storm into the kitchen and wondered what had upset him. He hadn't been happy when she'd insisted on calling her parents, but he'd given in with apparently good grace. She leaned back against the couch cushions and sighed. She had absolutely no experience with men, other than as colleagues. No wonder she couldn't figure Marcus out.

He came into the room and sat in a chair on the other side of the room. His gaze was cool and shuttered, and she had no idea what he was thinking. Finally he said, "Tell me about yourself."

She gave him a quizzical look. "What do you want to know?"

For a moment his gaze was hot and hungry, as if he wanted to devour her. She was certain he was going to say, "Everything." Then he shrugged and slouched in the chair, his eyes once again unreadable. "Who you are. What's important about Jessica Burke. Anything you want to tell me." He hesitated, then added, "Anything that could help us in this situation."

Pain squeezed her heart, but she wouldn't allow him to see it. If, after last night, he were only interested in helping her out of this dilemma, then she would deal with it. She wasn't going to die of a broken heart.

"There isn't much to tell you," she said, the coolness of her voice matching his. "I've been in school for almost my whole life. That pretty much is my life."

He leaned forward, a flicker of interest in his eyes. She suspected that he didn't realize it. "You're awfully young to be working on a Ph.D. already, aren't you?"

She shrugged self-consciously. "I suppose I am. But I've been pretty focused on my studies, so I progressed quickly."

He studied her, then nodded. "I thought so. Modest as well as brilliant."

She laughed. "That's not how I would describe myself."

"How old were you when you graduated from college?"

"Eighteen," she said, after hesitating.

"Precisely." He grinned at her, much of the tension gone from his face. "You were one of the brains in school, weren't you?"

Jessica felt her face tense, and she looked away. Those words still had the power to wound her. "So they say," she answered lightly.

Before she noticed him move, he was sitting on the couch next to her. "I'm sorry," he murmured, and he wrapped his arm around her shoulders. "That hurt, didn't it? And I didn't mean for it to hurt."

She forced herself to face him. "I know you didn't, Marcus. You couldn't know."

"Do you want to tell me about it?"

She shook her head. "No. At least not right now."

He leaned away from her so he could see her face. "I guess having money doesn't solve all the problems in the world, does it?"

His voice was light and teasing, and she tried to answer him in the same way. "No, it doesn't. But it helps when you go to the grocery store."

He moved away from her, but he didn't get up from the couch. And he didn't let go of her hand. "Speaking of groceries, I'm going to have to get some food together for us. We could get room service, but if I begin ordering two meals all the time, someone might wonder who's staying with me." He gave her a lazy grin. "Now, if I order two meals only occasionally, they'll just think I'm having a good time on my vacation."

"What do you suggest?" She tried to keep her voice as light as his, but the reference to his having vacation flings made a lump swell in her throat. Was that all she was to him? He was far more than that to her, but she would be damned if she let him see it.

He jumped up and began to pace around the room. "I don't want you out of this cabin, at least for now. I don't want anyone to see you." He stopped and spun to look at her. "Do you think you could describe the two kidnappers to an artist who might be able to draw them?"

"I think so." Their faces were burned into her mind.

He stared out the window. "It would help if I knew who we were looking for," he murmured, almost to himself. He was still for another long moment, and his stillness seemed to fill the room. The dancing sunlight that streamed through the window silhouetted his tall, rangy body and glinted off his blond hair. When he ran his fingers through his hair, she remembered how his hands had felt the night before, exploring her body, touching her everywhere.

As heat spread and pooled, she deliberately looked away. She didn't want to make more of a fool of herself than she already had. But his stillness and silence made her turn to look at him.

He was staring at her again, but this time his eyes were anything but cool. His gaze devoured her, made her feel like she was standing in front of him stripped to the skin.

"Jessica," he groaned, and she sat frozen in place, unable to move, unable to breathe.

The chirping of the cell phone shattered the tense stillness in the room.

Chapter 5

Marcus held her gaze for what seemed like an eternity. Finally, he moved to the phone and picked it up. But he never took his gaze away from her.

"Waters." His voice was curt and short.

He listened for a long time, then nodded once. "Thanks for the update. Everything is calm here. No signs of anyone snooping around. But she hasn't been outside the door yet."

He listened for a few moments longer, then said, "I'll need your help later today. I'll call."

He turned the phone off without saying goodbye, then put it down. "That was one of my partners. They haven't seen or heard anything at all about your kidnapping. And they've been to all the logical places on the island."

"What do you mean by logical places?"

His face relaxed, and she realized that he welcomed her questions. They defused the tension that threatened to explode between them. "They know all the seedy dives on Cascadilla, the kinds of places that lowlifes and scumbags hang out. They've visited all of them, talking to people and just listening. There hasn't been a whiff of talk about your kidnapping."

She watched him pace. "How is it that you know all the dives on Cascadilla if you're only here for a vacation?"

He stopped pacing and looked at her, reluctant admiration on his face. "You're very quick, Jessica."

"So I've been told. But that doesn't answer my question."

This time he grinned at her. "And persistent. I'll have to remember that."

"Just answer the question, Marcus."

His eyes actually twinkled, and she blinked as she watched him. Was this the intense, brooding man she'd been watching all morning? But as she watched him, his laughter faded. "That's a fair question," he said quietly. "A few of my partners are also vacationing here in Cascadilla. As soon as I realized that something had happened to you, I telephoned them and asked them to keep their ears open—unofficially, of course. They are married to the job—just like I am—and they agreed to forfeit some time on the beach to help me out. They tried to gather information as quickly as possible, and the places they went are the best sources. And to answer your question about how they knew where to go, it doesn't take much to find out where the scum on the bottom of the gene pool spends its time. Any taxi driver can tell you that. And once you find the dives, all it takes is money and time to get the information you need."

"You sound very cynical, Marcus."

He smiled again, but there was no humor in his eyes this time. "That's me, Jessica. I'm cynical and hard. That's why I don't belong anywhere near a woman like you. That's why what happened between us last night was so wrong."

"Nothing about last night felt wrong to me." She lifted her chin. "And what exactly is a woman like me?" She gave him a defiant stare, but she didn't really have to ask. A man like Marcus wouldn't be interested in an inexperienced woman like her.

"A woman with her life in front of her. A woman who could have any man she wanted. A woman who isn't tainted by the world I live in." Marcus held her gaze steadily. "An innocent."

"I'm not as innocent as you think I am."

"Not anymore, you're not. And that's my fault."

"It isn't a matter of fault," she retorted. "It was a matter of choice. And I make my own choices."

His gaze softened. "You don't know what you're saying, Jessica. You're still too caught up in the moment. But when you can think about this rationally, you'll see that I'm right."

"Don't patronize me. You're treating me like a child, Marcus. And I'm not a child."

"Damn right you're not." His gaze was suddenly dangerously hot. "And before I forget all my good intentions, I'm going to get out of here."

He stalked into the bedroom and closed the door. Jessica sat and stared after him, shaken by the heat that had flared between them. She had no idea how to handle the tension that stretched tighter every time they faced one another. Nothing she had read or studied had prepared her for the emotional storm raging inside her. Maybe agreeing to stay with him hadn't been such a good idea, after all. Maybe she should have called the Cascadilla police.

But she knew she wouldn't. She was going to stay here with Marcus and play this out. She had made her decision the night before, and she wasn't about to turn tail and run at the first sign of trouble.

That wasn't her way, in her personal life or her professional one. As a scientist, when she hit a snag she worked at it until she figured it out. And she was certain she could do the same with the mystery that was Marcus.

But she had never been so personally wrapped up in a scientific problem before, she thought, bringing her knees to her chin and wrapping her arms around her legs. She stared blindly out the window at the bright blue Caribbean sky. Somehow, she didn't think the scientific method was going to discover the real Marcus.

Her thoughts were interrupted by the click of the bedroom door opening. She swung to face Marcus as he walked into the room.

"I need to go get some groceries," he said, and once again his face was unreadable. "I called a couple of my partners. They're going to keep an eye on you."

"I don't need a baby-sitter," she retorted. "I'm perfectly capable of staying in this cottage by myself."

"They won't be in here with you." His voice was infuriatingly calm. "They'll be outside, watching the building. You probably won't even know they're around."

She tried to hide her worried expression, but she knew that Marcus could tell she was apprehensive.

"Do you mind if I leave for a while?" he asked. "I can stay here and ask someone else to pick up groceries for me, if you'd like."

"What if I said I did mind?"

"Then I wouldn't leave." His answer was prompt, and his eyes softened. She wondered if he realized it. "I won't leave you alone if you're nervous, Jessica."

"Go ahead and go," she said. She probably needed some time alone to regain her equilibrium. It had been thoroughly shattered the night before. "I'll be fine."

"Are you sure?"

"Positive."

His gaze lingered on her for a few moments, almost as if he couldn't bear to leave her. But that was ridiculous. Then he nodded. "Let me make sure my partners are in place."

He picked up the cell phone and took it into the other room. She heard the low murmur of his voice, although she couldn't make out the words. She let the sound wash over her, his voice bringing back memories of the night before. Images of Marcus in the moonlight filled her head, causing her pulse to quicken.

When he walked into the room, she opened her eyes and looked at him. He froze, staring at her, and she could see desire, tightly leashed, in the depths of his blue eyes. Then he looked away.

"There are two men outside. They'll make sure no one comes near this cottage until I get back."

"All right." She swallowed hard, trying to hide her reaction to him. "How long do you think you'll be gone?"

At that he smiled, erasing the tension that had begun to gather. "It shouldn't take long. There's a small grocery store on the grounds of the resort."

"I'll expect you soon, then."

He started for the door, then hesitated. "You're sure you'll be all right here alone?"

"Positive," she said firmly. "Go ahead and go."

"Anything in particular you'd like to eat?"

"I'm not a picky eater. Although I'm not too fond of red meat."

"No thick steaks, then."

"No. Anything else is fine."

He nodded once and slipped out the door. When the door closed silently behind him, Jessica wanted to run to the window to watch him until he disappeared. But she forced herself to stay where she was. She wasn't an adolescent with a crush on the cutest guy in the school. She was an adult, and that's the way she'd act.

Marcus strode away from the cottage, resisting the impulse to turn and take one last look. He wasn't a randy teenager, for God's sake. He was a professional, and he would damn well act that way.

He melted into the foliage next to his cottage and found the agreed-upon meeting place. After a few minutes another agent joined him.

"Devane," Marcus said in a low voice. "Any news?"

Russell Devane shook his head. "Not a whisper. Either your kidnappers aren't here on Cascadilla, or they're sharper than we've given them credit for. They're lying low."

"They're here on Cascadilla," Marcus said grimly. "And they're probably following Simon's orders and staying out of sight until they have an idea of what happened to Jessica Burke.''

''I did a background check on her and her parents, like you requested. They're legit, apparently. Her father has piles of money, both inherited and earned through shrewd investments. Jessica is completely on the level. School records are genuine, all the way back to elementary school. We had someone go to every school and check them out. Even saw pictures of her. And her academic adviser speaks of her in glowing terms. Can't wait for her to return to school.''

Marcus scowled. He wondered who her academic adviser was and why he was so hot for her to get back to school. ''So there's no chance she was planted by Simon?''

''I don't think so.'' Devane looked at him quizzically. ''Did you really think she was?''

''It doesn't matter what I think. The facts and the truth are all that matter,'' he snapped.

Devane raised one eyebrow. ''Someone didn't get enough sleep last night.''

Marcus glared at Devane to conceal the heat that flashed through him. ''Some of us are trying to catch Simon.''

''Man, you are as touchy as a boil.''

''Sorry.'' Marcus sighed. ''This business with Simon has been going on for far too long.''

''You're right,'' Devane said grimly. ''I say it stops here. We're going to catch that son of a bitch if it's the last thing we do.''

''Can you get us an artist?'' Marcus asked abruptly. ''She got a good look at both the kidnappers. If we knew what they looked like, we'd at least have a place to start.''

''I'll find someone.''

''Keep a close eye on the cottage,'' Marcus said, moving away. ''I'm going to get some groceries.''

''I could have done that,'' Devane said.

Marcus turned to look at him. ''I needed some fresh air. I'll be back as soon as I can.''

He pushed through the heavy foliage until he emerged on one of the paths that wound through the resort. What he'd needed was to get away from Jessica for a little while and regain his composure. He wasn't used to losing control the way he had the night before, and he was still shaken by what had happened between them.

No matter how much he wanted her, he would stay away from Jessica from now on. He was supposed to be protecting her, for God's sake. He had to have his mind clear and be able to focus on his job. And last night, he hadn't been focusing on anything but Jessica.

He wasn't able to focus on anything but her whenever they were in the same room. And that was a problem. He had promised he would protect her. He wasn't going to be able to do that if all he could think about was making love to her.

It wouldn't happen again, he vowed. He'd made a mistake, but it wasn't too late to correct it. From now on, he would stay as far away from Jessica as he could in the tiny cottage.

It didn't take long to find the grocery store tucked into a corner of the resort. After he stocked up on groceries, throwing items into the cart almost at random, he headed toward the cottage. The sky was a bright, cloudless blue, and the air was warm and sweet against his skin. He didn't care. He and Jessica weren't going to be able to enjoy it. They were going to have to stay inside for the next few days and let Devane and the other agents hunt for Simon and the kidnappers.

He slowed as he walked past the large pool, carefully looking at every person in the area. Some people splashed in the pool, others reclined on lounge chairs, reading or sleeping. No one looked out of place. No one seemed to be watching him. There was no scent of fear or excitement in the air, no vibrations from a hunter.

Satisfied, Marcus continued walking. When he got to the part of the path that led to his isolated cottage, he turned the corner and stepped into the dense foliage to wait.

After a few minutes, he stepped onto the path and continued walking. If Simon or his henchmen were around, they weren't following him.

As the cottage came into view, he paused to watch it for a moment. A man swayed in a hammock on the beach, not far from the rear of the cottage. Marcus recognized him as one of the agents on Cascadilla. Devane, he knew, was hidden among the trees at the side of the cottage, placed where he would have a clear view of the front and side. Between them, the two agents had the place covered. Jessica was perfectly safe.

Still he hurried to get inside. "Jessica?" he called softly as he stepped through the door. "It's Marcus."

She came out of the bedroom. "That was a quick trip."

He set the bags on the counter. "It wasn't like I

had a long way to go or a lot of choices once I got there.''

"Let me help you put everything away.''

They worked in silence for a few minutes. Marcus was too aware of how close she was. Every time they accidentally brushed in the tiny kitchen, his skin burned. Heat built inside him, along with a fierce need that threatened to blot everything else from his mind.

Finally he pushed away from the counter. ''That's it. I think that will feed us for a few days.''

"It looks like we're set.'' She took a deep breath, and he watched the rise and fall of her chest beneath the thin T-shirt she wore. She turned to face him, her mouth open to say something, but no sound came out.

Her eyes darkened as she stared at him. He knew what she saw in his face—raw, urgent need. It was impossible to hide it. In spite of his vow, he wanted nothing more than to haul Jessica against him and devour her, starting with her mouth.

And she wanted him, too. He could see it in the depths of her eyes, in the way her breathing quickened, in the way her body swayed toward his. All he had to do was reach out to her.

Instead he closed his eyes and clenched his hands into fists at his side. He'd never had any trouble putting his job first before this. Now he tried desperately to remember Simon and all that was at stake.

"Thanks for getting some food,'' Jessica said, and although her voice was cool, he could hear an echo of hurt in her tones. "I hope you don't mind, but I started reading one of your books. I'll get back to it.''

"Be my guest,'' he managed to say.

He heard her go through the living room and into the bedroom. When she didn't come out, he opened his eyes and looked out the window. The watcher in the hammock was gone, and he assumed that Russell Devane had left, also. Once again, he and Jessica were completely alone.

That helped to steady him. He was the only one responsible for her safety now. So he took a deep breath and waited until his desire was only a smoldering heat below the surface.

"Would you like some lunch?" he called to her.

"Yes, I'm getting hungry." She emerged from the bedroom, her face carefully blank. "Let me help you make something."

They worked together in silence for a while, but he realized that she was careful to keep the counter between them. Apparently she was just as wary as he was of those accidental touches.

They sat down on opposite sides of the table, and Marcus tried desperately to think of a safe topic of conversation. He wanted to ask her about her academic adviser, the man who was so eager for her to return to school, and he scowled. Their relationship wasn't any of his business.

"Tell me about your research," he said abruptly. "What do you do?"

She looked at him and raised an eyebrow. "Are you sure you want to know?"

"Of course I do." And he realized that he was telling the truth. He wanted to know what made her tick. He wanted to know everything about her. It was only so he could judge how she'd react in a crisis, he told himself.

"How much do you know about coral reefs?" she asked, her earlier coolness gone and her eyes sparkling as she leaned forward, elbows on the table and her food forgotten.

He shrugged. "Just that they're supposed to be beautiful."

Her eyebrows snapped together in disbelief. "You've never seen a reef?"

"Never had the time." Or the inclination, he should have added, but that was no longer true. Now he was very interested in them. He wanted to see them through Jessica's eyes.

"You're in the perfect place to fix that." She swept her hand toward the ocean. "There is a wonderful reef off the shore of Cascadilla. That's one of the reasons I wanted to stay at my parents' to work on my thesis. I had research material right at hand."

"What exactly are you studying?"

She grinned at him, and the tension that hummed between them vanished. That was a good thing, he told himself. "I'll give you the short version," she said, her eyes laughing. "I don't want to see your eyes glaze over if I start describing my research in detail. Basically, coral reefs are very important resources for humans. Reefs support an incredible amount of life. There are all kinds of things waiting to be learned about reefs, but we're causing a lot of damage to them. Increased environmental temperature, agricultural runoff and overfishing are just a few of them. I'm working on indicators that will allow us to know very early when a reef's been damaged so we can stop the damage and reverse the process."

"That sounds pretty complicated."

"It is. That's what makes it so interesting."

He could have sat across the table from Jessica for hours, watching the animation in her face as she talked about reefs and her work. "Can you be more specific?" he asked. "What are you doing?"

She hesitated, giving him a cautious look. "Stop me if I get carried away."

"Don't worry, I'm not a scientist. If you start throwing big words at me, I'll throw them right back."

"It's a deal."

Her meal forgotten, she started talking. Her hands fluttered in the air as she talked, describing the shapes of the coral she loved. In spite of the fact that he was telling the truth, that he was no scientist, he was enthralled by what she said. Not only was she doing complicated work, but she had the knack of describing it so he could understand. And he was fascinated.

Finally she faltered to a stop. "I warned you not to get me started," she said with a sigh. "I've bored you."

"I wasn't bored at all." It was the truth. "I enjoyed listening to you."

"Well, you know more than you probably ever wanted to know about coral reefs."

"I've heard enough that I want to see one for myself."

"I'd love to take you out to a reef," she said eagerly. "We can snorkel if you like. You won't get as good a view, but you don't need any special training."

"I've learned to scuba dive. I've just never used it." It was one of the things they had to learn during their training as SPEAR agents.

She frowned. "Why would anyone go to the trouble of learning to dive and then not use it?"

"It goes with the territory," he said dryly. "There

are a lot of things I've had to learn, like how to deliver a baby, that I've never used.''

"Of course. I had forgotten your job.''

She had forgotten everything but her work, and it was fascinating to watch. He cursed when a shadow appeared in her eyes.

"I had forgotten all about why I'm here," she said in a small voice.

"You can show me a reef when this is finished," he said recklessly.

"All right.''

But he saw the doubt in her eyes and realized how perceptive she was. It shook him to realize how well she could read him already. When this job was finished, he needed to run as far and as fast as he could. He wasn't ready to let anyone get that close to him. The last time he had, it had almost destroyed him.

He wouldn't think about that. He wanted to see the excitement in Jessica's eyes again. "No wonder you didn't have any trouble swimming from that boat to the shore. You must spend a lot of time swimming.''

"I did.'' She looked out the window as the sky darkened into dusk, and he couldn't miss the longing in her eyes. "I love the water. I miss it already.''

He couldn't bear that look of longing in her eyes. "I have a solution for that. Do you want to go swimming tonight?''

Chapter 6

"How could we do that?" He saw the excitement she tried to hide.

"Easy. We walk out the door of the cottage and into the water. The beach is right there."

"I thought it was important that no one see me."

"It is. But once we're in the water, no one is going to be able to see who we are. And when we're done swimming, we'll come back into the cottage."

He was being foolish, taking a chance he shouldn't take. But he always took chances. He ignored the fact that this one had nothing to do with his job. It would please Jessica, and suddenly, overwhelmingly, that was all that mattered.

No one was watching the cottage. Devane was sure of it. And they needed some exercise. Swimming at night, in the ocean, was a relatively safe way of getting it.

And a way to defuse the tension that still simmered

between them. If he swam until he was exhausted, he wouldn't be tempted to repeat the mistakes of the night before.

"If you think it's safe, I'd love to go for a swim." She jumped up and looked out the window. "We have to wait until it's completely dark, though, don't we?"

"That would be the safest."

Night fell quickly in the tropics during the winter months, and the sun had already set. Shadows lengthened, and the sky turned a deep, velvety blue. Finally it was dark enough to hide their escapade.

"Ready to go?"

"Yes." She gave him a brilliant smile. "I can't wait."

"Then let's go."

Before opening the front door, he listened for a while. He heard nothing but the normal evening sounds of the resort. The soft murmur of voices drifted through the air. People were heading toward the restaurants and bars that stood in the center of the resort. No one was coming toward the cottage. It stood by itself, isolated and close to the beach.

He opened the door and looked around, but didn't see a soul. "Okay, let's go," he whispered.

Jessica came up next to him clutching two towels, and he took her hand in his. She curled her fingers around his, a gesture of complete trust. If he were smart, he would have stayed in the cottage. But weighing the odds, he had decided it would be better for them to swim than to sit around inside all night, thinking about what had happened the night before. He glanced at Jessica, wondering what she was thinking.

*   *   *

Jessica clutched Marcus's hand as they stepped out the door and tried to rein in her excitement. She felt like a kid again, sneaking out of the house at night with her brother for some childish adventure. But her feelings for Marcus were anything but sisterly.

She had a good idea why he'd wanted to go swimming. She'd been able to see it in his eyes. It had been hard to ignore the tension that tightened between them with every look. Marcus wanted to put some distance between them, and what better way to do it than by exercising?

She didn't care. She had been restless and edgy all day, and swimming was the perfect way to dissipate her energy.

The sand was cool and smooth on the bottoms of her feet, and the air was warm and fragrant. The ocean was calm, the surface glinting in the light of the rising moon. She could already imagine how it would feel against her body, cool satin gliding against her skin.

Marcus started to pull off his shirt, and she stopped dead. "I forgot that I don't have a swimsuit."

He looked at her, and even in the dim light of the moon she could see his eyes gleaming. "Is that a problem?"

She had never swum naked in front of a man, but there was a first time for everything. She could add it to her list of firsts with Marcus. As he watched her, she slowly shook her head. "I guess not." Her breasts tingled, and a throbbing started low in her abdomen.

"I'll turn around."

"Thank you." She swallowed a huge lump in her throat and slowly took off her clothes, folding them into a neat pile on the sand. The warm air caressed her skin, and she shivered, suddenly feeling far too vulnerable. "I'm ready," she called, and fled into the water.

She saw a flash of pale skin as Marcus raced to the water's edge, then she turned and ducked under the water. When she emerged, she saw Marcus only a few feet away from her.

"We need to stay close together," he called. "I know you're a strong swimmer, but this is the ocean and we have to be careful."

"I know." She looked at the night sky, felt the waves gently lifting her and closed her eyes. "This is heaven."

All the fear and anxiety of the past twenty-four hours washed away in the rocking of the water, and she floated for a long time, watching the stars above her. When she finally turned over in the water, she saw Marcus treading water close by, watching her.

"You love this, don't you?" he asked quietly.

"More than just about anything." She glanced at his too-serious face again and slapped her hand on the water, sending a fine spray into the air. "I'll race you out to the buoy."

She flipped over and started swimming, getting a head start. But before long, he was cutting through the water next to her, his powerful strokes pulling him ahead. She stroked harder, finally drawing even with him. They were side by side as they reached the buoy.

"A tie," she said breathlessly. "You're pretty good, Marcus."

"I was about to say the same to you." She could see the respect in his eyes. "You're quite a swimmer."

"I get plenty of practice," she said easily. She hooked one arm over the buoy and floated on the waves, being careful to stay under the water. In spite of what they had shared the night before, she was still too conscious of her lack of clothing.

Marcus watched her steadily, and she wondered what he was thinking. The night shadowed his face and hid his eyes.

A strange tension hummed between them, buzzing along her nerves and making her mouth dry. Finally she said, "I'm going to swim for a while." She forced herself to smile. "But I'll take it easy on you. No more races."

"Go ahead. I'll keep an eye on the shore."

She swung her head around to scan the deserted beach, dark and shadowed in the moonlight. "Did you see something?"

"No, and I'm not expecting to." He finally moved, and she could see his face. It was all angles and planes, hard and unyielding. "It's second nature to me."

She eased away from the buoy and studied him. "Is it hard to live like that?" she asked, her voice quiet. "Always watching, always prepared for trouble?"

"It's what I've chosen." His voice was flat and final, but there was pain behind his words. She wondered why. Now wasn't the time to ask, but she wanted desperately to know.

As she watched him, she thought his face softened. "Go ahead and swim," he said gruffly. "You may not get another chance."

She turned and dove under the water, gliding through the darkness as the water wrapped around her like ribbons of silk. She swam for a while then floated, staring at the stars in the velvety tropical sky. Marcus stayed close, but never came within touching distance. And she was careful to stay under the water.

Finally her feet touched the sandy bottom. She felt around gingerly with her foot, wondering what she might find. "Marcus?" she called in a soft voice.

He swam over to her immediately, although he kept at arms' length. "What is it? Did you see something?"

"No, just a question. Have you been swimming here before? Do I have to worry about stepping on a sea urchin or a clump of coral?"

"No." His low voice seemed to wrap around her, his deep, husky tones reaching out to caress her. "It's just a sandy bottom. I think the resort keeps it cleared for swimming."

"Thanks." She put both feet on the bottom and started to stand up before she realized that she would be half out of the water if she did. She stumbled backward and lost her balance.

"What's wrong?" He grabbed her upper arms to steady her.

"Nothing. I just realized that the water is too shallow."

"Too shallow?"

She tried to move around him and stay crouched below the water level at the same time. "Too shallow to stand up."

"Oh." His hands tightened on her arms, and she stumbled backward, bumping into him.

Heat seared her as she slid along the long, cool length of him. When she tried to move away, his hands tightened on her arms and drew her closer. "Just for a moment," he whispered.

He pulled her against him, nestling her back against his chest. His coarse chest hair tickled her skin, and the heat of his body warmed her in the cool water.

Liquid fire raced through her veins, and she wanted to turn and press herself against him. But when she moved to do so, he crossed his arms beneath her breasts and held her still. "Don't move," he whispered.

She leaned against him and realized that he was heavily aroused. She froze, not sure what to do. If she had more experience, she thought wistfully, she would know.

Marcus seemed to read her mind. He bent, kissed her neck and whispered, "It's all right, sweetheart. Let me show you what to do."

He eased himself between her legs, so it felt as if she was riding him. When she moved once, tentatively, he groaned in her ear. She moved again, and he tightened his grip on her. "Hold still," he said, his voice hoarse. "I want to stand here with you for a while."

He nuzzled his face into her neck, then raised his head and searched for her mouth. She turned her head and kissed him eagerly, opening to him. He groaned again, and his hips jerked against her.

She ached with the need to turn around, to feel her breasts pressed against him. He must have read her mind, because he reached up and cupped her breasts in his hand. When he brushed her nipples with his thumbs, she gasped into his mouth.

She moaned when he moved his mouth to her neck. When he bent lower and took one of her nipples in his mouth, she cried out. He moved against her, sliding across her sensitive flesh like hot silk, and she sobbed, "Marcus!"

He raised his head, kissed her neck again and slid one hand to her belly. She felt the imprint of every one of his fingers burning into her skin, then he moved against her again.

She felt herself gathering, tightening, and she whimpered his name, mindless with need. He glided across her aching flesh again, and she exploded, spasm after spasm shaking her. She sagged limply against him, and he finally turned her to face him.

"I didn't mean to do that," he whispered. "I only wanted to hold you. But I can't resist you."

"I don't want you to resist me," she said fiercely. "And I don't want this to be one-sided." She reached down and touched the hard length of him. "It's not nearly as much fun alone."

He jerked away from her touch. "I don't have any protection with me," he said. "And I won't risk you that way."

"Then let's go get some protection." She leaned back until she could see his face, and she was startled at the pain she saw there.

"I swore I wouldn't touch you again, Jessica," he said in a low voice. "What happened last night shouldn't happen again."

"Why not?" Her voice was fierce.

"Why not?" He ran his fingers through his hair and gave a short, disbelieving laugh. "Where do you want me to start?"

"Wherever you like." She leaned against him, comforted by the contact. He could argue all he wanted, but she could feel the evidence of his desire for her.

"First of all, you barely know me. Hell, you don't know me at all."

"I feel like I know a lot about you already."

He ignored her words. "And secondly, I'm far too old for you. You belong with someone closer to your own age, someone who's not as cynical and hard as me."

She squirmed against him suggestively. "Maybe I like the fact that you're hard."

She felt laughter rumbling in his chest, then he leaned back and framed her face with his hands. "I don't deserve you, Jessica. And that's the best reason of all."

"Why don't you deserve me?" she asked quietly.

At first, she didn't think he would answer. Then he said with a sigh, "I'm fourteen years older than you. I've seen too much ugliness in my life and done too many things I'm not proud of. My soul is stained, Jessica."

"That's your job." She held his upper arms, as if to keep him close to her. "That's not who you are."

"My job is exactly who I am."

"I don't know why you'd say that, but it's not true. I've seen the real Marcus in the last twenty-four hours." She kissed him again and wound her arms around his neck. "Are you ready to go back to the cabin? It's getting a little cold here in the water."

She wasn't cold at all, but she knew that he would avoid going to the cabin for as long as he could. He'd keep as much distance as possible between them, then he'd hustle her into the house and into the bedroom, shutting the door firmly between them.

She was determined it wouldn't happen that way.

He bent and kissed her again, then he moved away from her. She smiled as her first prediction came true. "Let me take a look on the beach."

Marcus moved away from her, reluctant to break contact but determined to do the right thing. And the right thing was to stay away from Jessica.

He'd gotten carried away this evening, but he hadn't been able to resist her. She had been like a wild creature of the sea, swimming and diving, twisting and gliding through the water. He hadn't been able to take his eyes off her. And the longer he watched her, the more he wanted her. Finally, when she had innocently bumped into him, he hadn't been able to stop himself from reaching out for her.

It shouldn't happen again. And he would try to prevent it from happening again. He'd given everything he had to offer to Heather, all those years ago. He wasn't sure he had anything more to give. But God help him, he didn't know if he would be able to stop himself from touching her.

When he was far enough away that she was out of reach, he turned his attention to the beach. It looked deserted. He stared toward the shore for a long time, watching the shadows, trying to see if any of them moved. When he was satisfied they were alone, he turned back to Jessica.

"Let's go," he murmured.

She nodded, apparently knowing they needed to be quiet. She waded out of the water, and he saw only a flash of naked skin as she ran to the towels and wrapped one around herself. He tightened again as he watched her graceful movements.

He slung the other towel over his shoulder and took

Jessica's hand. Her skin felt cool to the touch and slick with salt from the sea. As they slipped around the cottage, he paused in the shadows next to the building and listened.

She stood motionless next to him, barely breathing. He glanced at her with approval, then let his gaze travel over the trees close to the cottage.

He bent his head to her ear. "When we get to the door, I'm going in first. You stay close behind me."

She nodded, and he leaned away to look at her. There was complete trust in her face, and very little fear. His gut twisted at the sight. He wasn't sure he wanted her to trust him completely.

But he couldn't think about that now. Taking her hand again, he led her to the porch. After listening at a window, he opened the door and slipped inside, Jessica right behind him.

Nothing looked out of place in the cottage. Nothing looked disturbed. He stood in the living room and listened, then nodded. It took only a few moments to search the rest of the cottage. No one had been in the house while they were out.

"It's okay," he finally said, reluctantly letting go of her hand. "No one's been here."

She stood in the middle of the room, the towel wrapped around her and her wet hair hanging down her back. Her eyes glowed. "Can we do this again tomorrow night?"

He had a feeling she was asking about more than swimming, and he scowled at her. "We'll see what's going on. We don't want to make anything a habit."

"Fair enough." She gripped her towel more tightly. "I'm going to put some clothes on."

"Why don't you take a shower?" he said, trying

not to look at her. "The salt on your skin might make you itch."

"Good idea. It'll only take me a minute." She beamed at him and hurried to the other room.

An uneasy feeling crept over him. It didn't sound as if she was planning on going to bed after her shower. He wondered what she was thinking. It didn't matter, he told himself as he grabbed a pair of shorts and a shirt. He'd let a moment of madness seduce him in the water, but he wouldn't touch her again. He knew better than that.

But she came out of the bedroom less than fifteen minutes later, and he wanted her all over again with a wave of desire almost too strong to resist. Her face was scrubbed clean, and she wore one of his T-shirts. He refused to let his gaze wander lower than her neck. It was obvious that she wore nothing beneath the flimsy cotton shirt.

"I borrowed one of your shirts," she said cheerfully. "I hope you don't mind."

"Not at all." His voice was sour, and he cleared his throat. "I'll try and get you some more clothes tomorrow."

"Don't worry about it. I don't mind sharing."

I do, he wanted to yell at her. Seeing her in his T-shirt was the worst kind of torture. It made him remember the night before and how powerful their lovemaking had been.

"You must be tired," he said, trying to keep any emotion out of his voice. "Why don't you go ahead and go to bed? I'll sleep here on the couch."

The cheeriness faded from her face, and she looked at him steadily. "Is that what's known as a brush-off?"

"Dammit, Jessica, one of us has to have some sense here." The words exploded from him. "I was completely out of line last night, not to mention what happened in the water just now, and you know it as well as I do. So we'll both just forget it happened."

"What if I don't want to forget about it?" She didn't let her gaze waver from his face.

He closed his eyes, unable to bear the longing he saw in her face. "You have no idea what you're saying."

"Look at me, Marcus," she said sharply. He reluctantly opened his eyes. "Do I look like a child? Do I look like someone who doesn't know her own mind? Do I look like I can't make decisions for myself?"

"No, Jessica, you don't, and you damn well know it," he sighed.

"Then why are you treating me like I am?"

"Because I'm trying to do the right thing here. I'm trying to do what I should have done last night and stay the hell away from you."

"Why is that?" Her voice was soft.

"Because it's not fair to you. Because I can't guard you when I'm not paying attention." *Because I don't want to let you any closer than you've already gotten. You've already gotten too close to the barriers I need to protect myself.*

He saw the mischief lurking in her eyes. "If you're concerned about keeping me safe, I'd say you couldn't get much closer than sleeping in the same bed."

"That's the problem. There wouldn't be much sleeping if we were in that bed together."

The impish look faded from her face. "I know

that,'' she said quietly. ''I knew that when I asked. But if you're not interested, all you have to do is say so.''

He saw the uncertainty on her face, the vulnerability in her eyes, and he suddenly understood. She had no experience with men, especially with men like him. She was afraid that he'd found her lacking last night. He groaned and reached for her.

''Sweetheart, it's not that.''

''It's not what?'' She leaned away from him to look at his face.

''It's not that I don't want you.'' He closed his eyes and pulled her close. ''I want you more than I can ever remember wanting anyone.'' *Or anything.* ''I'm just trying to do the right thing for you.''

''And what gives you the right to decide what's right for me?''

''I'm trying to be a gentleman here.''

She snuggled against his chest and put her hand over his heart. He was sure she could feel it pounding against her fingers. ''I don't think you're a gentleman,'' she said thoughtfully. ''Am I right?''

He groaned. ''I've never been accused of that before. But I'm trying.''

''I don't think I want to make love with a gentleman.'' She lifted her head, and he opened his eyes to look at her. ''I want to make love with you, Marcus.'' Her voice faltered and lowered to a whisper. ''Did you mean it when you said you wanted me?''

His heart kicked in his chest. He knew how hard it must have been for her to ask him that. ''Yes, Jessica. More than you know.''

The tightness in her face eased and changed to a brilliant smile. ''Then let's go to bed together.''

She turned toward the bedroom, but Marcus tugged at her hand until she turned and faced him. "I want you to know, Jessica, that if you want me to stop, all you have to do is say so. I swear it."

"I know that." Her smile faltered, and he could see the nerves behind her bravado.

"I know this is all new for you." He reached out and brushed a damp tendril of hair off her face. He wanted to tell her that it was new for him, too, that he felt things for her that he'd never felt before. But he couldn't find the words, so instead he bent and kissed her.

Chapter 7

Marcus pulled her close, the need that was never far from the surface when he was with Jessica spiraling dangerously out of control. He'd never felt such urgency, never wanted a woman the way he wanted her. And she was kissing him as if she felt the same way.

"Are you sure?" he whispered. He had to give her every chance to make the wise choice.

"What do you think?" She opened her eyes to look at him, and their amber depths were drugged with passion. "Believe me, Marcus, I'm not usually this forward."

She had taken a chance, made herself completely vulnerable, because of him. His heart kicked again, and he tightened his arms around her. "I won't hurt you, Jessica."

"I know," she whispered.

Whatever else happened, she would be safe with him, he vowed. And when the moment came to return to their own worlds, as he knew it would, he would let her go and wish her only the best.

But for now, she was his. He bent to kiss her again, and she wrapped her arms around his neck and opened her mouth to him. Tenderness washed over him, and he scooped her into his arms and carried her into the bedroom.

He smoothed his hands down the T-shirt she wore, absorbing the heat from her skin, feeling her tremble as he touched her. Need for her raged inside him, but he refused to let it control him. Jessica had been a virgin until last night, and he was determined to be gentle and patient.

But when she turned into his caresses, her arms reaching for him, his good intentions evaporated. He had to see her, to touch her. When he slipped his hands beneath the thin cotton, she murmured his name and blindly reached for him.

"Jessica," he groaned, burying his face in her neck, breathing in her scent. "I need you."

"I need you, too," she whispered, and when he looked down at her, he saw that her cheeks were stained a delicate pink. His heart surged in his chest. He knew damn well she'd never said those words to another man, and a fierce sense of possession gripped him.

"I want to see you," he murmured.

She started to pull the T-shirt over her head, but he could see her hands trembling. He reached down and kissed her hands, then covered them with his. "Let me."

Slowly he pulled the shirt up and over her head, then he dropped it on the floor. She was completely naked on the bed, the moonlight dappling her body with mysterious light. "You're beautiful," he whispered, then realized that she wasn't quite meeting his eyes. His heart melted at the sign of her nerves. He sat up to peel off his clothes. "It's only fair if you get to look, too."

She gave a shaky laugh. "You must think I'm an idiot."

"I think you're wonderful." He tossed his clothes on the floor. "Look all you want."

She let her gaze wander over him, then reached out and touched the fresh scar on his arm. "What happened?"

"I had an accident."

"A car accident?"

"It doesn't matter now. It's almost completely healed."

Her fingers brushed over the scar, lingering for a moment, then she bent her head and kissed it. "I'm sorry."

"Don't be," he said, his body tightening with desire. "Just touch me again."

She smoothed her hand over his chest, then brushed against the tense muscles of his abdomen. He sucked in a breath, but didn't move. When she hesitated at his heavy arousal, he had to close his eyes to keep from reaching for her. "Marcus," she breathed, "may I touch you?"

"Touch all you want. Please."

They had come together in an explosion of need and desire the previous night. Tonight, he vowed, he was going to give her all the time she needed.

Instead of moving below his waist, she brushed his chest with a butterfly-light caress. Her hand slowly moved toward one of his nipples, and he felt himself tense. When she touched him lightly, a bolt of lightning sizzled to his groin. He grabbed the sheet to keep himself from reaching for her, and she bent down to touch him again. Her hair tickled his chest, then he felt her tongue gently touching his nipple.

"Jessica," he groaned, and she raised her head.

"Does that feel as good as when you do it to me?"

He was trembling all over with the struggle to control himself. "I don't know. Let's find out."

If he didn't touch her, he would die. It was as simple as that. He raised himself onto his elbow and eased her onto the bed. When he took her nipple into his mouth and suckled, she cried out and clutched at him.

"Marcus," she panted as he slid his hand down her belly and cupped her. "I wasn't finished exploring you."

"I wouldn't have been able to take another moment," he said grimly. "You have no idea what you do to me."

"Tell me." She opened her eyes, and he saw they were two dark pools of need and hot desire. "Tell me, Marcus."

"I want to show you."

The need to join with her was pounding in his head, firing his blood, blocking out everything else. And when he moved between her legs, she welcomed him with a tiny murmur of happiness deep in her throat. He barely had time to protect her before he surged into her.

She moved with him, wrapping her legs around him, murmuring his name. And when her movements became more frantic, he buried his face in the fragrant mass of her hair and allowed his control to slip.

Their cries blended together in the silence of the room, and they lay together for a long time, holding each other and murmuring soft words. When he tried to shift to the side, to take some of his weight off her, she tightened her hands around him. "No, don't," she said, and her voice was sleepy and drugged with pleasure. "Don't move."

"I'm not going anywhere," he said. He rolled to the side and pulled her close. "I won't let you go."

She gave a murmur of satisfaction and snuggled against him. "Now I know what all the girls in my classes in college were talking about," she said in a sleepy voice. "I always thought they were silly to talk about sex all the time. I don't anymore."

"Didn't you ever want to find out for yourself?" He idly stroked her hip and breathed in her fragrance.

"I was too busy. And I never met anyone I was seriously interested in."

He lifted onto his elbow and stared at her. "Why was that? I thought that meeting members of the opposite sex was part of the college experience."

"Maybe for you, but not me." She was silent for a moment, then turned to face him. "I was the youngest in all my classes, and I was very insecure, at least socially. It was a lot easier to concentrate on my studies than take a chance on dating. So I stuck with what I knew I was good at."

"You never dated in college?" he asked, staring at her.

"I graduated when I was eighteen," she said. "For most of the time I was there I was way too young to date, anyway."

"What were your parents thinking of?" he demanded. "Why did they send you off to college when you were so young?"

"It was my choice. I told you, I was smart and I wanted to play to my strengths." She looked away. "I guess maybe it was a way to avoid social situations, too. Since my father had money, dating was hard. My parents always warned me that men would be after me for my money. So it was difficult to trust a guy's motives."

"Jessica, look at yourself in the mirror sometime. There's your motive right there."

She gave him an odd little smile. "You don't care at all about my money, do you, Marcus?"

"Why should I? I have all the money I need."

"That's what I thought." She smiled again and closed her eyes. "Your motives are pure."

"My motives are as impure as they can get." He pulled her against him so she could feel that he was hard again. "Should I prove it to you?"

"Not yet." She gave him a slow, simmering look. "I was exploring you, and I never got a chance to finish."

"Be my guest." His heart began pounding again, and desire tore through him. "I promise I'll be more patient this time."

"I think I like it when you're impatient," she murmured. Then she touched him and drove all thoughts of patience out of his head.

Jessica woke up to feel the sun pouring through the window at the top of the room. Marcus was sleeping beside her, one arm curled around her, and she closed her eyes and allowed herself to revel in the happiness of the moment.

"We're both lazy this morning," he said into her ear.

She turned to him as if it was the most natural thing in the world. "I blame it on lack of sleep. We were too busy with scientific experiments last night."

"Is that what you call what we were doing?" He lifted himself onto one elbow and looked at her with a lazy grin.

Her heart swelled in her chest. "I had certain gaps in my knowledge, and we worked together to fill them," she said, trying to sound dignified.

"I think I just found another gap," he said, reaching for her. "Come on over here while I take care of it."

He kissed her thoroughly, and she felt herself melting into his embrace once again. But when she whispered an endearment, he froze, then moved away and sat on the edge of the bed. "I'm going to take a shower," he said abruptly, and vanished into the bathroom.

When he emerged ten minutes later, he didn't look over at her. "I'll get some coffee started."

"Okay." She watched him as he left the room, wondering at his abrupt change of mood. She might not be a virgin anymore, she thought as she walked into the bathroom, but she sure didn't know a lot about men. As she stood under the hot water, she tried not to feel hurt. He was right to focus on their problems. Marcus was trying to help her, she told herself. He was trying to help catch her kidnappers so she could go back to her life.

But suddenly that life didn't seem nearly as attractive as it had two days ago. As soon as it was safe for her to return to her family's island, Marcus would take her home and disappear. And she would never see him again.

She'd worry about that later, she told herself firmly. Right now, she had to worry about more important things. And she had to make sure Marcus wasn't suffering from an attack of guilt over the night before.

She finished her shower, put her clothes on and wandered into the living room. Marcus had made a pot of coffee, and he was standing next to a window, drinking from a mug and staring outside.

"See anything?" she asked lightly.

He turned to face her. "Not a thing. We're safe so far, and I want to keep it that way. Would you mind if a couple of people came to the cottage today? I'd like you to work with an artist and see if we can come up with sketches of the two kidnappers."

"That would be fine," she said. "How soon can they be here?"

His eyes softened. "Thank you," he said softly. "I'll call them now."

He picked up the cell phone and dialed a number. "It's me. Any time is fine." He listened for a moment, then said, "Good."

After he closed the phone, he said, "They'll be here in about a half hour."

"Then I guess I'd better have something to eat," she said. "It sounds as if I'll be busy for a while."

An expression she found hard to read chased across his face. "You're being a real trouper about this, Jessica."

"What were my other options?" she asked. "Throw a fit and demand to be taken home? What good would that have done?"

He gave her what looked like a reluctant smile. "It's what a lot of people would have done."

"I guess I'm not a lot of people."

"I'm beginning to realize that," he murmured, watching her, another odd expression on his face. "Let's get something to eat before the artist gets here. It could take a while."

It took more than two hours, but by the time the artist was finished, they had pictures of both kidnappers. Jessica stared at them and felt the hair rise on the back of her neck.

"That's them," she whispered. She looked at the artist, a woman who hadn't spoken except to ask her questions about the kidnappers' features. "You've done a remarkable job."

"Thank you," the woman said briskly. She glanced at the two men who had accompanied her. "Anything else?"

The taller of the two men shook his head. Jessica had noted that Marcus didn't introduce her to any of the trio. "That's it. We'll get going." He turned to Jessica. "Thank you for your cooperation, Ms. Burke. We appreciate it."

"You're welcome."

Marcus studied the pictures, ignoring the three people who stood near the door. Finally he looked at her. "You've said this man—" he gestured at one of the pictures "—worked for your father. Anything else you remember about him?"

She stared at the picture for a long time, then shook her head. "No." She gave him an apologetic look. "I was really wrapped up in my work for the last few weeks. I hardly noticed my parents, let alone the people who worked on the island."

"How about this guy?" He held up the other picture. "Ever see him before he grabbed you?"

She shook her head again. "He doesn't look familiar at all. And believe me, I've given it a lot of thought."

"Okay." Marcus stared at the pictures. "And it was this one, the one you'd never seen, that seemed to be in charge?"

"Yes. He's the one who was giving the orders. He's the one who talked about the man named Simon who wouldn't be happy if they made any mistakes."

Marcus stared at the pictures again, and she knew he was committing them to his memory. "All right." He handed the pictures to the taller of the two men, and he and the other two people left the cottage as silently as they had arrived.

Marcus waited until the door closed behind them, then turned to her. "They'll make copies and start to ask some discreet questions." He paused for a beat. "You have a remarkable memory for details."

She shrugged, although his casual praise made her stomach flutter. "It's my job. I have to remember details."

"And I'll bet you're damned good at your job."

"I try," she said lightly. She wasn't sure how to respond, so she changed the subject. "The artist was very good."

"She's got a reputation as the best. That's why I requested her."

"Why are you doing all this for me?" she demanded. "You told me that this Simon wanted to kidnap me for ransom. This is getting pretty complicated for a simple little kidnapping. Is there more to the story that you're not telling me?"

''I've told you the truth all along, Jessica.'' His eyes turned hard and unreadable. ''I found you on the beach and brought you back to the cottage. I was going to call the police until I realized that you were in danger. Do you want to call the police now?''

''No. I've told you I trust you and that I'll do what you think is best. But you're going to an awful lot of trouble for me.''

His eyes softened slightly. ''And why wouldn't I do that?''

''Because you don't know me and you don't know my parents.'' Her voice was blunt. ''What's in it for you?''

He watched her steadily, and she could see the sadness in his eyes. ''Doesn't anyone ever do anything for you unless there's something in it for them?''

She turned away, unable to bear the pity in his eyes. ''I guess a suspicious mind comes with having money,'' she muttered.

He put his hand on her shoulder, but she didn't turn around. ''Believe me, Jessica, money is the last thing I want from you or your parents. A reward of some kind is the furthest thing from my mind.''

She did believe him. But she noticed that he hadn't really answered her question. Turning, she said, ''Why didn't you introduce me to your partners?''

His face relaxed, and he shoved his hands into his pockets. ''That's easy. If you don't know their names, you can't tell anyone that you met them.''

''But you said you worked in law enforcement. I don't understand why so much secrecy is involved. Why would it matter if I wanted to describe your partners?''

He sighed. "Jessica, the less you know, the better off you are."

She stared at him, trying to ignore the slightly sick feeling in her stomach. "This sounds way too melodramatic for me. Are you really implying that someone would hurt me to make me divulge information?"

"It won't come to that, I'm sure. But we're better off if I think in worst-case scenarios."

For a moment she wasn't sure she knew the grim-faced stranger who stood in front of her. "Who are you, Marcus?" she whispered.

"I'm nothing but trouble," he said bluntly, his voice cold. "I've told you all along that you shouldn't get involved with me." His face was hard and closed. "Your parents wouldn't approve of me. Hell, they wouldn't want you to get involved with me if I was the last man on earth."

"You've never met my parents," she said stiffly. "You're underestimating them."

"I doubt it. I don't belong in your world, Jessica." He stared her with a stranger's eyes. "Hell, if you need any more proof, we come from totally different universes. You graduated from college when you were eighteen, and I never even went to college. I went into the Army right out of high school. Your family has money, and I work in law enforcement. Do I need to go on?"

"Don't bother. I'm sure you have lots more to say," she said sweetly, her temper stirring. "I'm sure you could come up with excuses all day and all night why we're all wrong for each other. But last night sure felt right."

"You don't know anything about it," he said, and

his voice was harsh. "You were inexperienced, Jessica. You have nothing to compare me with."

"I don't need any comparisons to know what we've shared is very special. I know how I feel."

"What you feel is gratitude," he said sharply. "That's all."

"You can think what you like and feel what you like. But don't tell me what I think or feel," she retorted.

He stared at her for a moment, his eyes dark blue with frustration. She stared back, defiant, unwilling to back down. She had always fought for what she wanted.

The thought startled her. Did she want Marcus? She wasn't sure. Nothing was certain right now. Her world had changed and shifted, and she felt completely off balance. She looked away, unwilling to let him see the turmoil inside her.

"I'm going to check out the area," he said gruffly. "I'll be right back."

She watched him slip out of the cottage, not sure if she was sorry or glad he was gone. Ever since she'd met Marcus, she'd felt like she was falling off a cliff. Now she was afraid she was going to hit the bottom without anything or anyone there to cushion the blow.

But given the choice, she wasn't sure if she would turn the clock back, either. She was afraid that she would endure the terror of the kidnapping all over again if it brought her to Marcus. And that thought terrified her more than the kidnapping ever had.

Marcus stepped into the dense foliage near the cottage and took a deep breath. He wasn't escaping from Jessica, he told himself. He was leaving before he said or did something that he couldn't take back. He'd been right, no matter what Jessica thought. She didn't belong with him. She belonged in her own world, with people who shared her background. He'd learned long ago, after the disaster of his affair with Heather, to stick to women who understood who he was and what he did. And who understood that there wasn't any long term in his life. He'd made his choice when Heather had forced him to choose between her and his career. He'd chosen his career and now he would live with it.

But Jessica had cast a spell over him that he was powerless to resist. Every time he tried to tell himself she was too young for him, she managed to convince him they fit together perfectly. Every time he tried to convince himself her money was an insurmountable barrier, she brushed it aside as if it was nothing. And he was afraid that if he spent any more time with her, he would agree.

So he would do his job, find her kidnappers and force them to lead him to Simon. This was his chance to catch the traitor, to end the turmoil within SPEAR once and for all. He wasn't about to be sidetracked by a woman, no matter how beautiful, no matter what he felt for her.

And what he felt for her was nothing more than overwhelming lust, he told himself. That's all he would allow it to be. If Jessica touched a part of him that he'd hidden for too long, she didn't have to know. He could ignore his feelings. He'd been doing it for years, after all.

Besides, it was ridiculous to imagine that he felt anything more than lust for Jessica Burke. It had only been a few weeks ago that he'd imagined himself in love with Margarita Alfonsa de las Fuentes.

A voice inside reminded him that most of Margarita's appeal was that he knew she was safe. He knew that Margarita was in love with Carlos, and although she was fond of him, they would never be more than friends.

Marcus slapped the spiny bark of a tree and turned away from the cottage. He hadn't come out here to moon about Jessica. He could do that very well inside the cottage. He'd come out here to check the surroundings, to make sure that no one had found them during the night.

Because he sure as hell wouldn't have known if a whole squadron of men had surrounded the house while they slept last night, he thought sourly. He'd been far too involved with Jessica, far too busy making love with her.

He forced himself to concentrate on the area around him. The cottage was set apart from the others for a good reason—privacy. SPEAR didn't want anyone to be able to watch the comings and goings from the cottage when it was being used in a covert operation. But the isolation made the cottage a more inviting target.

He'd searched yesterday and found nothing. But they were only safe as long as he was vigilant. So he searched again.

And stopped abruptly about fifty yards from the cottage. Someone had sat here last light. Branches were broken. Leaves were crushed and pressed into the earth. Marcus rocked on his heels, staring at the evidence. Someone had sat here, possibly watching the cottage, while they made love last night.

Chapter 8

He took a deep breath and warned himself not to jump to conclusions. An animal could have made the marks. Or a guest of the resort could have been there for some very innocent reason.

But it wasn't his job to embrace the innocent explanation. It was his job to assume the worst. So he stood slowly and looked around the area. After a long time, he let out the breath he'd been holding. No one was there now. He was certain of that. No one watched him. No one waited to spring out of hiding.

He needed to spend some time, to examine the area closely and make sure there was no other evidence. But he couldn't leave Jessica alone in the cottage any longer. Especially now.

He loped to the cottage and burst through the door. He couldn't stop his sigh of relief when he saw Jessica sitting on the couch, reading a book.

"What's wrong?" she asked, jumping off the couch.

"Why do you think something's wrong?"

"I can tell by the look on your face," she said impatiently. "What is it?"

No one else was able to read him so instantly or so accurately. A shiver ran up his spine, but he ignored it. He didn't have time to examine the phenomenon right now.

"Did you hear or see anything while I was gone? Anything out of the ordinary?"

"Not a thing," she said, watching his face. "I've been sitting here reading your book the whole time."

He glanced down and saw that she had picked up one of his suspense novels. "Did the phone ring?"

"No." She laid the book on the table. "What is it, Marcus?"

He saw the beginnings of fear in her face and reached for her hand. "It's probably nothing. But I found a place in the foliage not too far from the cottage where someone or something had been sitting."

"Someone was out there watching the cottage?" she asked.

She was quick, he thought with a burst of admiration. "It's possible."

She sank onto the couch. "What do we do now?"

"We don't panic," he said, sitting next to her. "There could be a perfectly innocent explanation. I'm going to take a closer look at the area and see if whoever was there left any clues. Then I'll have my partners come out this evening and keep an eye on the area."

"What can I do?"

"You can stay in the cottage and out of sight."

"Won't it go more quickly if both of us are searching?"

"You have no idea what to look for."

"Then tell me." She took a trembling breath, then squared her shoulders. "These people are looking for me. Staying here with you has put you in danger. I don't want to sit inside while you take all the risks. Let me help you."

Again he felt a surge of admiration. "Most people would be happy to stay inside and out of the way."

"Then I guess I'm not most people," she retorted. Her eyes softened. "And besides, why should you have all the fun?"

"This isn't my definition of fun," he said.

"I know." She reached over and touched him, and he wanted to take her in his arms. Instead he clenched his hands. "But I want to help." She quirked a grin at him. "Maybe you could use my analytical skills."

"This isn't a game," he said, his voice grim. "If these men find you, they'll try to grab you again. Or worse."

"I know that. But I trust you to take care of me." Her voice was calm and her gaze direct. "I'll put you up against those two losers any day of the week."

"Those two losers, as you call them, managed to snatch you very neatly from a private island with a security system. We have to take them seriously."

"Then let me help you look for evidence," she said immediately. "Two sets of eyes will work faster and more efficiently than one. And besides, is it safe to leave me here in the house by myself?"

He watched her for a long time, but her gaze didn't waver. Finally he said, "You play dirty, don't you?"

"It depends on how badly I want something. And I want to help you."

He thought for a moment. She was right; he didn't want to leave her alone in the cottage while he searched through the dense tropical growth. Part of his attention would always be here instead of on what he was doing. And she had another valid point. Maybe two sets of eyes were better than one.

"All right, you can come with me. But you have to do exactly as I tell you."

"Absolutely." She jumped up from the couch. "Let's go."

"Not so fast. I have to call my partners and let them know what's happening."

He grabbed the cell phone and walked into the bedroom, shutting the door behind him. He really didn't need privacy to make the call, but he needed some distance from Jessica. He couldn't concentrate when she was watching him. All he wanted to do was hold her and tell her that he would keep her safe.

Russell Devane answered the phone, and Marcus quickly told the other agent what he had found. "I'm going to look around now, but it might be a good idea if you have someone in the woods tonight, in case they show up again."

"I'll be there." Devane's voice was quietly confident. "Let me know if you find anything." There was a pause. "What about the woman? Are you going to leave her alone in the cottage while you're searching? Do you want me to come over and sit with her?"

"I'm taking her with me." Marcus's voice was flat and uncompromising. He didn't want to think about why he wouldn't trust Jessica's safety to anyone else.

"I don't want to wait for you to get here and I don't want to leave her alone."

"Fine. I'll be in the woods tonight. You stay in the cabin."

No more skinny-dipping in the dark, Marcus thought as he closed the cell phone. The ache of regret was hard and fast. But it had been a dangerous idea from the very beginning. In more ways than one. He closed his eyes as he remembered her responsiveness, the eager way she had surged against him, clutching his hands and pulling him closer.

Maybe staying inside tonight wasn't such a bad idea, after all.

When he opened the door and walked into the tiny living room, Jessica was pacing the room. "Are we ready to go?" she asked when she saw him.

"Just about." Marcus hurried into the kitchen and stuffed some plastic bags into his pocket. Then he reached into a drawer, pulled out his gun, tucked it into the waistband of his shorts and covered it with his shirt. "Let's go."

Her eyes were wide as she stared at the place where his gun was concealed. "Are you sure you need a gun?" she asked in a small voice.

"I hope not, but you never know." He leashed his impatience when he saw the fear on her face. She wasn't a part of his world, he told himself. Why would she take his gun for granted? "Are you sure you wouldn't rather stay here?"

She shook her head. "I'd rather be with you."

Pleasure bloomed in his chest, and he immediately tried to squash it. "Then let's go."

They slipped into the screen of trees that lined the path outside the cottage. It was like they'd stepped into another world. Dim, greenish light filtered through the canopy of leaves, and the heat and humidity became oppressive. The breeze that kept the beach comfortable couldn't penetrate the vegetation, and the air was heavy and hot.

"It's hard to believe this is part of the same resort," Jessica said in a low voice.

"What do you mean?"

"The rest of the resort is so civilized. This is elemental. It makes it hard to forget that Cascadilla is mostly a rain forest."

"The resort wants you to forget that," he said, his voice dry. "They've done a lot of work to make it seem like a tropical paradise, but they can't completely get rid of the jungle. It's surrounding us."

"And that's good for the kidnappers, isn't it?"

"They can use it to their advantage," he said slowly, looking around at the remnants of the inhospitable jungle. "But then again, so can we."

"What do you mean?"

"We're going to turn the hunters into the hunted. And those pictures you helped draw are the first step."

She stopped and turned to look at him. It felt like she was assessing him. Finally she smiled. "I don't think I'd want to be hunted by you, Marcus. I have a feeling that you don't lose too often."

He'd lost in Madrileño, he thought sourly. Not only had he lost Margarita, but he'd lost Simon, as well. And if he was being truthful, he regretted Simon far more than Margarita.

He slanted a glance at Jessica. Especially now.

"Those kidnappers of yours are playing it smart.

Apparently they're laying low. My partners haven't heard even a whisper about your kidnapping.''

And that was because of Simon. He was certain of it. Simon would keep a short leash on his employees. He'd know that the surest way for them to get caught was to let them go to the dives of Cascadilla and allow liquor to loosen their tongues.

''Then what makes you think they were here in the trees?'' she asked in a low voice. Even though they were in the middle of a patch of jungle, both of them seemed inclined to speak in hushed voices.

''Right here,'' he said, pointing.

She squatted to look more closely. Finally she glanced at him, her eyes troubled. ''It does look like someone was here. But aren't there animals that live in the jungle? Why couldn't it have been an animal lying here?''

''It could have been. But we can't afford to assume that. We have to assume only the worst.''

''All right. What are we looking for?''

''Why don't you look for something that doesn't belong here? Candy wrappers, gum wrappers, soft drink bottles or cans, cigarette butts. Anything like that.''

''What are you going to be looking for?''

''I'm going to try and figure out where they came from and how they left.''

They worked together in silence, the only sounds the hum of activity from the resort. It seemed far away and in another world. Marcus made sure that Jessica was never out of his sight, and at first he watched her work.

She was careful and methodical, and he noticed that she went out of her way to disturb the area as little as possible. In short, she did everything he would have done himself, he was forced to admit.

"You're doing a good job," he said gruffly.

She turned her head to look at him. "It sounds like you don't want to admit it."

"There are too many things I like about you already, Jessica." He spoke without thinking, then wanted to snatch the words back.

Her eyes softened as she rocked on her heels and faced him. "I think that's the nicest thing anyone has ever said to me." Her voice was a throaty murmur in the semidarkness, and her eyes gleamed. "Thank you, Marcus."

"Don't let it go to your head." His voice was rougher than he intended, and he could hear the fear beneath his words. He didn't want to feel anything for Jessica beyond keeping her safe and using her to catch Simon. "I'm sure it's your training as a scientist."

"I'm sure it is." He heard the laugh beneath her voice and scowled at her. She didn't sound offended by his words. If anything, she sounded amused. And that scared him even more.

He had no business being interested in Jessica Burke. She was way out of his league, in more ways than he could count.

He could blame it on proximity and adrenaline, but he was too honest for that. The truth was, she fascinated him. Everything about her interested him. When they were able to ignore the sexual tension that always hummed beneath the surface, they could talk for hours. And rather than dreading the next few days, when they would be spending a lot of time together, he was looking forward to them.

Thank God she would be going back to her world as soon as they caught her kidnappers. He wasn't sure how much restraint he was going to be able to exercise. Especially since she seemed to want him as much as he wanted her.

"I've found something," she called in a low voice, and he cursed himself for lapsing into a daydream.

"What is it?" He scrambled to join her.

"Take a look. I'm not sure."

He crouched beside her, and she pointed to a sodden, pulpy mass of paper. Taking a stick, he poked at it until he was able to turn it over. Then he pulled one of the plastic bags out of his pocket and slipped it inside.

Once it was protected, he examined it from all angles. Jessica stared at it, murmuring, "I wondered what those bags were for."

"It looks like the packaging from some kind of snack food," he said slowly, trying to flatten it and read the writing on the paper. "I don't think it's going to help, but we'll hang on to it anyway. How did you find it?"

"I was pushing aside the dead leaves," she answered. "It was beneath them."

He nodded, staring at the spot she indicated and mentally measuring the distance from the crushed vegetation. "It's probably not from whoever was here last night. But it was a good find." He gave her what he hoped was an impersonal smile.

"Why don't you think it was from whoever was here last night?"

"Because it's too old. It's been outside for a long time. Anything from last night would be a lot fresher."

"And it probably wouldn't be hidden beneath the leaves, either." Her voice was full of disgust. "I should have thought of that."

"At least you found something," he said. "Let's keep going."

But after another hour he was forced to admit that there wasn't anything to find. "Let's call it a day," he finally said. "There isn't anything here."

She stood and stretched, and he tried to look away from the sight of her body, illuminated by the dim, mottled light. But he couldn't do it. Her breasts strained against her shirt, and her skin seemed to glow. It took all his self-control not to stand up and reach for her.

She looked at him and froze. They stared at each other for what seemed like an eternity. Finally he stood and deliberately looked away.

"Let's go get something to drink," he said, his voice hoarse.

"That sounds good."

Her breathing sounded harsh, like she'd been running. A fierce jolt of desire washed over him, and he took a deep breath and closed his eyes as he struggled for control. This was dangerous, he told himself harshly. God only knew who was close by.

"Let's go."

She walked with him toward the cottage. He didn't dare look at her, but he was still too aware of her presence. Her scent surrounded him, faint but alluring. It managed to block out the moist smell of the jungle. And his skin crackled with electricity every time he brushed against her as they walked between the trees.

* * *

Jessica looked at Marcus walking beside her. Tension emanated from him like a coiled spring, ready to explode into action. She wondered if it was because he had found something in the woods or because of the moment that had passed between them. She'd turned to find him staring at her, hunger in his eyes. And an answering hunger had swept through her.

Whatever it was, she was certain he wasn't about to tell her. She waited until they were inside, then turned to confront him. "What did you find out there?"

He seemed startled by her question. "Nothing. I told you that."

"Then what's wrong?"

He turned to face her. "What the hell do you think is wrong?" His eyes glittered, and his face was taut with passion. "I can't keep my mind on my job. That's what's wrong."

"Oh." She stared at him, stunned that she could inspire such passion in a man. Especially a man like Marcus Waters. She was caught in the pull of his gaze, lost in the hot depths of his brilliant blue eyes. "If it's any consolation," she said softly, "you make me forget why I'm here, too."

He closed his eyes, and she could see the struggle for control on his face. Finally he opened his eyes. "Don't say things like that to me, Jessica. I'm having a hard enough time keeping my hands off you."

She opened her mouth to answer, and he held up his hand. "Don't say it. We both know that it's dangerous and stupid to get so involved with each other."

"I don't know any such thing," she said hotly. "I think you're just afraid to get close to anyone."

She saw a flicker of pain deep in his eyes, then he

shuttered them. "You're right that I'm afraid to get involved with you. I told you I'd protect you. I'm doing a hell of a job, aren't I? You weren't in this house more than four or five hours and you'd lost your virginity."

"Why do you keep harping on that?"

"Because it's important."

"It's only important if I say it is. I made a choice, too, Marcus. It wasn't all one-sided."

"You were frightened and stressed. I took advantage of you."

She sighed. This was a battle she wasn't going to win. "There's nothing we can do about it now, is there? So why not forget about it?"

"Because every time I look at you, I want to make love with you again. And I have to concentrate on keeping you safe."

Her heart leaped at his words, but she tried to face him calmly. "All right, then, we'll leave the love-making question for later. What did you think about what we found in the trees?"

She watched him shifting gears, fascinated by the way he was able to instantly shut off the emotional, physical part of himself. "You mean what we didn't find?" he asked sourly.

"Isn't that just as important as what might have been there?"

"Yeah," he conceded. "It means one of two things. Either whoever or whatever was in the woods last night was nothing to worry about, or your kidnappers are smarter than we thought."

"And which do you think it is?"

"I told you, I always like the worst option. And after what they managed to do on your father's island,

I have to think your kidnappers are pretty damn smart.''

"But couldn't it have been an animal?"

"That's possible. But we have to assume that it wasn't."

She shivered at the thought. Was it possible that someone was outside this cabin last night while they made love? Was it possible that someone would be back tonight, waiting for an opportunity to harm them?

"What do we do next?"

"Not a thing. My partner is going to be in the woods tonight. If someone comes back, he'll find them."

"I guess that means no evening swim," she said wistfully.

His eyes softened. "I'm afraid not. At least not until we know who was out there."

"I guess we'll have to find another way to amuse ourselves, then," she said mischievously.

"There are plenty of books in here," he said. "Or we can watch television."

"Or we can just talk. I like talking to you, Marcus."

She saw a yearning in his eyes, quickly hidden. "I enjoy talking to you, too," he said gruffly. "You have an interesting view of the world."

"And so do you," she retorted.

Surprisingly, he grinned and held up his hand. "Not now. I have some things to do."

He reached for the phone that was never far from his hand and dialed a number. "It's me," he said. "There was nothing in the area."

He listened for a while, then said, ''Sounds good. We'll be here.''

He folded the phone and set it on the table. ''One of my partners will be watching the cottage tonight. We'll be safe.''

''You sound like you trust him completely.''

''I do.'' His face closed, and she realized he wouldn't talk about his job.

''Thank him for me the next time you talk to him,'' she said.

His eyes softened. ''I'll do that.'' His gaze lingered on her for a moment, then he looked away. ''Are you hungry?''

Clearly the discussion about his job and his partner was over. ''Starving,'' she said lightly.

''Then let's find something to eat.''

They spent the rest of the day in the cottage. Every once in a while, Jessica glanced out the window at the endless blue of the sky and wished momentarily that she were out enjoying the beautiful weather. But then she would look at Marcus and smile. She was perfectly happy inside, sitting with him, talking and reading. She discovered that Marcus could discuss books, world politics and sports with equal knowledge and passion. And she found herself leaning forward, eager to hear his opinions and discuss her own.

Time flew by, and before she knew it, the sky outside the window was turning a dark, velvety blue.

She leaned back and curled her arm around the sofa to stop herself from reaching for him. ''I enjoyed myself this afternoon.''

''I did, too.'' He seemed startled to realize it.

She smiled as she stood and stretched. ''I think it's time to eat again.''

After they ate, they sat in the living room, each of them reading a book. Jessica found herself straining to hear, listening for sounds from the trees near the cottage. But all she heard was the faint sounds of music and laughter that came from the resort's restaurants and lounges.

"You're not going to hear anything," Marcus finally said.

She glanced at him. "What do you mean?"

"There could be a war outside the door and De…my partner will make sure it's a silent one. We don't want to attract any attention from the other guests."

"It's just so hard to wait."

"I know." She could see the sympathy in his eyes. "Why don't you go to bed? You didn't get much sleep last night."

She caught his gaze and held it. "Are you going to bed?"

"No. I'm going to wait for a while."

"Then I will, too."

They continued to read, although Jessica couldn't have said what was in her book. Finally, a little while after midnight, they heard the sound of soft footsteps on the porch and a quiet knock on the door.

Chapter 9

Jessica held her breath while Marcus peered out the window. She noticed that his hand hovered over the gun he wore in the waistband of his shorts. When he dropped his hand and pulled open the door, she let out the air in her lungs with a whoosh.

One of the men who had accompanied the artist earlier that day stepped through the door. He nodded to her, then looked at Marcus. "It's okay. You don't have to worry that Ms. Burke has been found, or about anyone watching the cottage."

Jessica saw Marcus's eyes narrow. "Are you sure?"

"Positive." The other man relaxed enough to allow a small smile to curve his lips. "Your mystery intruder was a couple, and they came back to the spot tonight. From what I heard, they're both single parents who are here on vacation with their kids. They needed a place to, um, get together, and they chose the woods. Apparently it's a lot more discreet than sending the kids out to the pool.''

She saw the amusement glittering in Marcus's eyes. ''I hope you left equally discreetly.''

''As soon as I realized what was going on.''

Marcus held out his hand. ''Thanks a lot, buddy. I appreciate it.''

''No problem. Call if you need anything else.''

''Will do.''

The other man slipped out the door as quietly as he'd arrived. She glanced out the window, but he had already disappeared into the shadows. When she turned to look at Marcus, he was watching her, his eyes hooded and brooding. He looked like a stranger, and a dangerous one, at that. Her heart skipped a beat, but she tried to act nonchalant.

''All that worry for nothing,'' she said lightly.

''It wasn't totally worthless,'' he said in a low voice.

''What do you mean?''

''It gave me an idea of how you'd react in a crisis.''

''I could have told you that.''

He shook his head. ''I doubt it.'' He glanced at her, and the hard look on his face eased. ''Or maybe you could have, but I wouldn't have believed you. I had to see for myself.''

''And do I pass?'' she asked, curious about his response.

''You know you do,'' he said, and his eyes pierced her with their intensity. ''You did exactly what I hoped you would do.''

''What is that? Stay out of your way?'' she joked.

He shook his head, his gaze steady on her. ''You

didn't panic. You used your head and were able to help me. You thought about what we needed to do. And you did what I asked, without questions.''

"Don't get used to that," she warned with a weary smile. Now that the danger was over, all her energy had leached away. "I like to ask questions."

"I've noticed." His gaze was unreadable. "But you didn't ask them today. And I appreciate that."

"Today was a little different. I figured I'd better leave it to the expert."

"You've surprised me at every turn," he said, watching her with a burning intensity. "I don't know what to make of you, Jessica."

"You pretty much get what you see with me," she said, shrugging.

The evening was taking on a surreal quality. Three days ago, she couldn't have imagined she would be having a conversation like this with her lover. Three days ago, she wouldn't have dreamed she would have a lover. It had been the last thing on her mind. And now she was sitting here in this cottage, alone with Marcus, discussing their expectations of each other.

He shook his head. "I don't think so. I've spent enough time with you to realize that." He shoved his hands into his pockets and whirled around to look out the window again. "We're stuck in this tiny cottage together twenty-four hours a day. And I can't think of another person, besides a fellow cop, I would rather have with me right now. That scares the hell out of me."

Her heart leaped, but she struggled to control her reaction. "This is all pretty new and strange for me, too," she managed to say in an even voice. "It's not exactly what I pictured myself doing when I decided to stay on the island with my parents for a few months.''

At that he turned and smiled at her. "It's not, is it? You thought you'd be doing your research and instead you're cooped up here with me, waiting for the bad guys to show up.''

She shrugged, longing to reach for him but knowing he would immediately retreat. "It's not so bad.'' She gave him an impish grin. "We got to go swimming, at least.''

His eyes darkened, and she knew he was thinking about what had happened last night, about the incredible lovemaking they had shared. "Yeah, we did, didn't we?''

His voice was no more than a low murmur in the stillness of the night, smooth and seductive. Desire leaped to life inside her, shocking her with its suddenness and power.

"Are you interested in another swim?'' she asked, barely recognizing her voice. She sounded like a stranger, husky, smoky and suggestive. She saw his face tighten and knew the desire she saw in his eyes was echoed in hers.

"I don't think so,'' he said after a moment. "Not tonight.''

"Why not?''

"Because I don't want to make love to you on the beach,'' he said roughly. "And that's exactly what would happen if I saw you in the moonlight.''

She held out her hand to him. "Then let's just go to bed.''

He held himself rigidly still. "That's not what I meant, Jessica.''

"I know. You think you know what's best for me. But you don't. I want to make love with you."

He shook his head, and a small smile curved his lips. "Say what you mean," he murmured.

"I always do."

"I've noticed." He reached out and touched her cheek, skimming one finger down to her neck. "It's hard to believe you're only twenty-one years old."

"Then don't think about it."

"I can't help myself," he said roughly, drawing his hand away and clenching it into a fist at his side. "I'm far too old for you, Jessica. In every possible way."

"And I think we're just right together." She tried to rein in her impatience. "I already told you that I found the boys my age far too young for me. Their preoccupation with drinking beer, chasing women and having a good time was boring. Why else do you think I've never had a serious relationship?"

"You said you were too busy to date."

She gave him a slow, heated smile. "Believe me, Marcus, if I had met you while I was in college, I would have made time."

"I've taken advantage of you," he said, his voice brutally frank. He watched her steadily. "I stole your freshness and your innocence. I've taken what I had no right to take."

"And I've already told you that I knew what I was doing. I don't want to have this conversation again. Give me credit for knowing my own mind." Her temper flared, and she glared at him. "I want to make love with you, Marcus. I have no idea how much time we'll have together. And I'm not going to argue with you every night. So make up your mind. I'm going to bed.''

She walked into the bedroom, leaving the door open behind her. She could feel Marcus's presence in the other room, knew he was watching her. Ignoring him, she went into the bathroom and closed the door.

When she emerged, there was no sign of Marcus. A lump swelled in her throat. She had taken a gamble and lost. Marcus was going to stay as far away as possible from her.

Fighting tears, she pulled on one of Marcus's old T-shirts and slid between the sheets of his bed. Rolling onto her side, she stared out the window and blindly watched wispy clouds track across the moon.

''I didn't think you were ever coming out of that bathroom,'' Marcus whispered as he slid into bed next to her.

She rolled over to face him. ''Where were you? I thought you had left.''

''I wouldn't leave you here alone without telling you where I was going. I was checking the outside of the cottage and making sure everything was secure.''

''Is everything all right?'' She was asking about far more than the security surrounding the cottage.

He stared at her for a long time. Finally he reached for her and pulled her into his arms. ''Everything is fine. For now.''

For now. She knew it was the most she could expect from Marcus. He wasn't prepared to make any kind of a commitment to her, at least while he was responsible for protecting her. But as she wrapped her arms around him, she promised herself that she wasn't going to let him go as easily as he thought. One of the barriers between them had come crashing down. He had taken a small step in her direction tonight, and it was all the encouragement she needed. Sooner or later, he'd find out that her stubbornness and persistence could easily match his.

Then his mouth came down on hers, and she forgot everything but the desire that swept her away. She forgot the danger she was in, she forgot her work, she forgot everything but Marcus and the passion they shared. For now, it was enough. And as he made love to her with a sweetness and a tenderness that brought tears to her eyes, she felt a piece of her heart break away and tumble into his hands.

The next ten days passed far too quickly for Jessica. She and Marcus spent their days talking and their nights making love with a passion and hunger she hadn't known existed. It was as if they'd been lovers for years, so perfectly did they fit together. Every once in a while she felt Marcus trying to retreat, to separate himself from her. But once he touched her, once he kissed her, all the barriers between them dissolved, and passion burned hotly between them again.

Marcus sat watching Jessica at breakfast two weeks after he had found her on the beach. Her movements were graceful, and she smiled at him, tenderness and caring in her eyes. He knew that his eyes would soften in response. Jessica was undermining all his defenses. She had become his world. He couldn't seem to get enough of her, and the realization made him edgy and tense.

This wasn't how he did his job. He didn't allow himself to get distracted while on an assignment, even if the woman doing the distracting was part of his job. Scowling, he pushed away from the table and grabbed the phone. He'd call Devane and see if there were any developments.

He felt Jessica's eyes on him, and he turned away and dialed the number. When Devane answered, he said, "It's me. Anything new?"

"Not a thing. We've been turning over every rock on Cascadilla, but nothing has crawled out yet. Anything to report from your end?"

"Nothing. It's been quiet as a tomb here."

"Something has to break soon. Especially if Simon was behind the kidnapping. If he needs money that badly, he can't afford to go to ground for too long. We'll keep our eyes open." Devane paused. "It might be time to shake things up a bit."

Marcus knew what he meant, and he scowled at the phone. "Not yet. It's too risky."

There was another pause. "Catching Simon is our first responsibility, Waters," Devane finally said, but Marcus could hear the sympathy in his voice.

"I know. I'll talk to you soon."

When he closed the phone, he turned to find Jessica watching him, worry in her eyes. "Your partners haven't found anything yet, have they?"

"No. But they will. It just might take some time."

"This waiting is hard for you, isn't it?" she asked softly.

"It's tough."

What was worse was the guilt that was tearing him apart. Deep down, he wasn't sure he wanted the kidnappers to be found. Because as soon as they were found and used to trap Simon, Jessica would return to her world, and he'd go on to another assignment in his. He'd be left with nothing but memories of the passion they shared.

And that was the way he wanted it, he reminded himself. There was no place in his life for a commitment to a woman. He couldn't ask a woman to share his life when he never knew from one day to the next where he would be. He was gone for months at a time, working on an assignment. Jessica deserved a man who would be there for her. And a man in his line of work wasn't who she needed in her life.

He abruptly began to clear the table. Jessica stood up to help him, then glanced at the phone. "What did you think was too risky?"

He didn't want to tell her, but he did anyway. "He wants to use you as bait. He wants us to parade around Cascadilla, to be as visible as possible. He figures that the kidnappers are watching for you. And if they see you, they'll come after you, and we'll have a chance to catch them." And Simon.

Instead of dismissing the idea, she stared at him, her eyes narrowed. He could see her thinking about the proposal, and he didn't like what he saw.

"Forget it, Jessica. It's too dangerous."

"Why do you think so?"

"What if something went wrong? What if we didn't catch them? What if they managed to grab you again? I'm not willing to take that chance."

"What if I am?"

"It's not your decision to make," he said harshly. "My partner and I have decided to wait them out."

"But they're not coming out, are they?" she replied. "It's been two weeks, and there hasn't been any sign of them."

"They'll have to come out eventually."

"Why? Maybe they've just gone off and kidnapped someone else."

"That hasn't happened."

"How can you be so sure?"

"It's my business to be sure of things like that. Believe me, we would have heard if there had been another kidnapping in the area. We're not going to use you for bait."

She raised her chin and glared at him, and his heart twisted in his chest. Jessica didn't take orders well. She insisted on knowing the reasons, insisted on an explanation. His Jessica was strong and stubborn, and that was one of the reasons he found her so attractive.

His Jessica? he thought with a tiny flare of panic. She wasn't *his* Jessica, and she never would be. She was the woman he was protecting. She was his key to catching Simon, and he'd damn well better not forget it.

But he wasn't about to risk her in the process.

"I think we should use me as bait," she said, and he could see the wheels turning in her head. His heart sank. After two weeks, he knew her well enough to know that once she got an idea in her head, she was more tenacious than a terrier with a bone.

"It's too risky. I don't want to take a chance with you," he said, feeling as if the words were torn out of him.

"I trust you, Marcus," she said quietly. "I know you won't let me get hurt."

"Things happen." His voice was harsh. "Not everything can be predicted. Not everything can be prevented."

She gave him a slow smile. "I'm perfectly happy in this cottage with you. I don't care how long we stay. But doesn't your vacation have to end sometime?''

He scowled at her but didn't answer. She was right. They had been living a fantasy life for the past two weeks. But sooner or later he would have to go searching for Simon again. The traitor could only wait for so long. He needed money to continue his campaign against SPEAR, and if he didn't get it from Jessica's parents, he would have to look elsewhere. And another chance to catch him would be gone.

"Let's go for it." She leaned toward him, her eyes sparkling. "Have you seen much of Cascadilla?"

"Not really. I was laid up with my arm when I first got here, and then I found you. So I haven't seen much beyond the resort."

"Perfect. We'll be tourists, and I can show you all the sights." She grinned at him. "We'll go snorkeling. I can't wait to show you the reefs."

"I didn't agree," he said, desperately trying to think of a reason to refuse.

But there wasn't a reason, and he knew it. The only reason was to protect Jessica, and he was brutally honest with himself. If it were anyone else, he would have used them as bait to catch Simon a long time ago.

Shaken at the realization, he turned away. "I'm going outside for a while. I won't go far."

He stepped into the balmy air and watched the tourists on the beach. Some were swimming, some sunning themselves and some lying in the shade, reading a book with a cool drink. None of them noticed him standing on the porch of the cottage.

His emotional attachment to Jessica was clouding his judgment, making him cautious where he should be bold. His first loyalty was to SPEAR, to catching Simon.

But he couldn't bear the thought of risking Jessica. His thoughts went round and round like squirrels in a cage. Before he had made a decision, he heard the door open, and Jessica came out and sat beside him.

"You're not thinking with your head," she said quietly. "We can't stay in this cottage indefinitely, as much as I would like to. You know that."

He turned to look at her. Her eyes shone with a steady light. "I don't want to spend any more of my time with you hiding in a cottage. I want to get this kidnapping behind me and get on with my life. With our lives."

Her meaning was clear to him. "There is no 'our lives' after this is over, Jessica," he said, and his voice was harsh. "I thought you understood that."

"I don't think this is the time to discuss it. And it doesn't matter, anyway. You know what we have to do."

"Yeah, I know." He turned to look at the beach. And it did matter. It was going to be the hardest thing he ever did, but he was walking away from her after this was all over. He owed her that. He had taken too much from her already, and he wanted to take far more. He had never met anyone like Jessica. His heart clenched when he thought about leaving her. But he had to do it.

And maybe that was why he was so reluctant to do as she suggested. Maybe, deep down, he knew that it was the beginning of the end. And God knew he didn't want what they shared to end.

"It'll be all right, Marcus. You'll keep me safe.

And once those kidnappers are behind bars, we'll be free.''

Once the kidnappers were behind bars, he would have to catch Simon. And he'd have to do it while guarding Jessica. He knew from bitter experience that Simon was as brilliant as he was evil. He'd do exactly the opposite of what anyone would expect. And Marcus refused to take a chance that he'd go after Jessica himself.

''Okay,'' he said, not looking at her. ''You're right. We don't have any choice. I'll call my partner and let him know what we've decided. Then we'll figure out our strategy.''

She gave him a smile, then leaned over and kissed him. Desire, which was never far from the surface with Jessica, exploded into life. He leaned over to kiss her again, and she melted against him.

Stay here with me, he wanted to whisper. *Let's ignore the world, Simon, the kidnappers, everything but the two of us.*

But he didn't do it. He couldn't. He'd promised to catch Simon, and he would. So he tore his mouth away from hers, slowly put some distance between them. If he didn't, they would end up in bed together.

And they had things to do. Jessica's eyes fluttered open. He saw the passion in their amber depths, the need, and he wanted to reach out to her. Instead he said, ''Hold that thought for a while.''

''I will.'' Her voice was smoky with passion and desire. She smiled at him, and his heart turned over in his chest. ''Just don't make me hold it for too long.''

It took all his willpower to stand up and extend a

hand to her. Pulling her to her feet, he said lightly, "Let me make that phone call."

He saw the flicker of disappointment in her eyes. Then she nodded. "I'll clean up from lunch."

The phone call to Russell Devane didn't take long. Devane breathed a sigh of relief. "Thank God you've come to your senses. It's about time you took her around Cascadilla. It's our only hope of drawing those two kidnappers out. And catching Simon."

"I know that. Just make sure you're around in case there's any trouble today."

"We'll be there. Where are you going?"

"Into the capital city," he said after thinking for a moment. "That's where the crowds will be. And being a city, it's the most likely place for the kidnappers to have gone to ground."

"We'll watch for you. Get a taxi to let you off at the market."

"Will do."

He snapped the phone closed and slipped it into his pocket. Then he retrieved his gun and slid it into the waistband of his shorts.

Jessica came out of the kitchen in time to see him do it. She stilled, a dish towel in her hand, and stared at him for a moment. Then she smiled brightly. "Are we all set?"

"As soon as you're ready."

"Where are we going to go?"

"Into the capital."

She nodded. "That's a good choice." She gave him a quick grin. "And I can get more clothes at the market. That way I won't have to keep wearing yours."

He liked to see her wearing his shirts. But he thinned his lips and nodded. This wasn't about what he liked. "Let's go, then."

Chapter 10

Jessica leaned back in the cab and watched the sights of Cascadilla flashing past. She had always loved the island, loved its colorful culture and friendly people. And under any other circumstances, she would have been excited about the prospect of showing the island to Marcus.

Although he had agreed to leave the safety of the cottage, he didn't seem happy about being here. He sat on the other side of the taxi, staring out the window. When he leaned forward, she could see the dark gray metal of his gun at his back.

It was a sobering reminder that they weren't on a pleasure trip. They were pretending to be tourists, on vacation and carefree, but the reality was far different. The smiling, gracious face of Cascadilla was a mask that hid an ugly truth. They were the hunted, and they would have to be constantly on alert. Her momentary pleasure faded. The terror of her kidnapping came surging back. Now she was deliberately putting herself in the way of those two men again.

"Nervous?"

Marcus touched her hand, and she looked over at him. "A little," she confessed.

"I'd be worried if you weren't." He squeezed her hand and gave her a reassuring smile, his eyes softening. She turned her palm over to twine her fingers with his.

"I keep telling myself that nothing could happen in the middle of a city. But I thought the same thing about my parents' island."

He brought her hand to his mouth, his lips lingering on her fingers. "We should be safe today," he said. "Even if they were to spot you, they wouldn't be expecting you and so they probably wouldn't have time to react. But from now on, we have to expect trouble."

"I know," she said, and she cursed the tremor in her voice. This was the right thing to do.

"There will be lots of people watching us," he said, tucking her hand into the crook of his arm. She held on tightly. "And they have the pictures. They know what the kidnappers look like. Don't worry, the two men who kidnapped you won't get close to us."

"I know that. And I know I'm being silly."

"You're not being silly," he said gently. "You're too smart not to realize the danger in what we're doing. And I'm sure this has brought back the memories of your kidnapping."

"It's hard not to think of it," she confessed. "Especially when we're trying to lure those two men out of hiding."

"I'll be here, Jessica. I won't let anything happen to you."

"I know." She trusted him completely—even though he hadn't wanted to do this. He'd been vehement about it. She wondered whether it was because it would mean the end of their time together. She hoped so, but didn't have the nerve to ask him.

But now that he'd decided they needed to be seen around the island, all traces of hesitation had vanished. He was a different man than the one who made love to her so tenderly every night. This Marcus was almost a stranger. He stared out the window with hard eyes, watching everything. His gaze was cold and calculated as he swept the area. A coiled tension emanated from him, winding more and more tightly as they approached the center of the city.

When the taxi stopped, he leaned forward to pay the driver, then turned to her. "I'll need to hold your hand all the time," he said rapidly in a low voice. "If you see anything unusual, squeeze my hand. Don't turn around and look or point."

She wanted to interrupt, tell him that she knew better, but the focused, intent look on his face stopped her. Marcus was a warrior, she recognized with a shimmer of awareness, and he was preparing to go into battle.

He had kept this fierce, elemental part of himself carefully hidden from her. Was it because he was afraid it would frighten her away? With a flash of insight, she realized that it was. She knew Marcus considered himself to be too old, too experienced for her. But it wouldn't have mattered. She'd been attracted to his strength from the very beginning. And she knew what kind of man was hidden beneath his fierce surface.

He was tender and loving, and so careful of her. He claimed he was satisfied with his solitary life, but she had seen the yearning and the need in his eyes when he thought she wasn't looking. Marcus needed her as much as she needed him.

And she was beginning to realize that she needed him far more than was safe or wise.

But right now they had to worry about more dangerous things, and she reluctantly focused her attention on their surroundings. Marcus accepted his change from the taxi driver, handed him a tip, then pulled her out of the car.

They stood in the street, and she looked around, trying to get her bearings. The crowds of people and the noise were almost oppressive. She moved closer to Marcus, and he smiled at her. But she could see his eyes watching everything around them.

"It's a little overwhelming," she said in a low voice.

"That's because you've spent the last two weeks isolated from the world. All this noise and all these people are a shock." He bent and pressed a quick kiss to her lips. "Give it a few minutes and you'll be fine."

"What are we going to do?" she asked.

"What would you like to do? Is there any place you'd like to go?"

He watched her patiently, and she realized that he was giving her time to steady herself, allowing her to set the pace. Tenderness swept over her. Even in such a tense moment, he was still thinking of her first.

She gave him a shaky smile. "Thank you, Marcus," she said quietly. "Why don't we walk in the market for a while?"

"That sounds like a good idea." He took her hand, then looked around. Anyone watching them would assume he was just trying to get his bearings.

"My partner is signaling," he said in a low voice. "They haven't seen a thing."

"All right." She licked her lips, drew a deep, unsteady breath and folded her hand into his. "Then let's go."

The market was two streets over, and they strolled casually in that direction. Marcus stopped occasionally to look in a store window. He would point out some trinket and smile at her, saying something innocuous, but she watched his eyes. He was using the reflections in the glass to check behind him. His eyes moved constantly, assessing and categorizing everything around them.

"Do you see anything?" she finally asked in a low voice.

He shot her a startled look. "Is it that obvious?"

"To me it is. But I doubt anyone else would realize how carefully you're watching."

"You weren't supposed to notice, either," he muttered.

"Marcus, I've spent the last two weeks with you. I've had nothing to do but talk to you and study you." Her voice was impatient. "Of course I know what you're going to do."

He turned to look at her, and there was a peculiar look in his eyes. "Two weeks isn't that much time."

It was long enough for her to know what she wanted. And she wanted Marcus.

The thought shocked her. Her step faltered, and Marcus slowed, glancing at her. "Are you all right?"

"I just stumbled," she answered quickly, keeping her face averted from Marcus. He would certainly be able to read the shock and surprise she was sure was in her eyes.

"How about an ice cream cone?" he said, pointing toward a small shop.

"That sounds good."

A few minutes later they walked out of the tiny store. Jessica licked her ice cream absently, her mind racing. She had always thought her career would be the most important thing in her life. She had planned for it, worked for it with a single-minded dedication that had her on the brink of receiving her Ph.D. at a very young age.

But that was before she'd met Marcus. Now she could think of nothing but him.

Maybe she was enthralled with him because he had shown her the passionate, physical side of herself. Maybe that was all it was.

But she knew it went far deeper than that. She knew she was fascinated by everything about Marcus, by the emotions and feelings that wove beneath his hard, tough exterior. Emotions he tried very hard to hide.

"You're awfully quiet." His voice interrupted her thoughts, and she licked her ice cream cone before she answered.

"I was concentrating on finishing this before the heat got to it." She scrambled to make her voice light and carefree.

"And here I thought you were thinking about me."

Her startled gaze flew to his face. Desire smoldered

in the depths of his eyes, and as she licked her ice cream again, she watched his face tighten.

A wave of answering desire swept over her, and she wished they were at the cabin. His eyes darkened. "Me, too," he whispered. He bent to kiss her, and she clung to him, kissing him back.

After a moment he stepped away. He still held her hand, and she could feel him shaking. "That's the last time I'm buying you an ice cream cone," he said, his voice throbbing with need.

"And here I was enjoying it so much."

"Yeah, I know. That's the problem." He brought their joined hands to his mouth and kissed her fingers one at a time. "But I need to enjoy it more privately."

"Is that a promise?" Her voice was shaky, and her legs felt wobbly. Desire flowed through her veins, sharp and sweet.

"You'd better believe it."

She could barely tear her gaze from his, from the promise in his eyes. Then a man stepped out from the alley ahead of them, startling her. She jerked to a halt and Marcus spun around, his hand reaching behind his back.

They stood frozen for what felt like an eternity, but was only a moment. Almost as if it was part of his quick movement, Marcus's hand fell away from his shirt, and he tugged her forward to begin walking again. The man who had appeared in front of them melted into the crowds and disappeared.

"What was that all about?" she asked, her voice low and still shaky with desire.

"That was one of my partners." His voice was grim. "He was reminding me to pay attention to what was going on."

"I'm sorry, Marcus."

"It's not your fault."

She looked at him and saw that he had shuttered his face, his eyes hard and unforgiving of himself. "It's not your fault, either," she said. "We just forgot."

"I can't forget what we're supposed to be doing, Jessica." His voice was harsh and angry. "If I do, you could get killed."

"It's all right. Nothing happened."

"Only because we were damned lucky." His face had settled into rigid, unyielding lines. "But don't worry, it won't happen again."

"Don't beat yourself up like this, Marcus," she said gently. "It was only a matter of a few seconds."

"That's all someone would need to kill you."

"Fine," she said, losing patience with him. "You go ahead and have a pity party for yourself. I'm going to look around the market. I need some more clothes."

He glanced at her, startled, and she gave him a hard glare. "I mean it, Marcus. You're not perfect, and neither am I. We made a mistake. The world didn't end. Now get over it."

His eyes glinted dangerously, but she refused to look away. Finally his eyes softened and his mouth twitched. "I guess I've been put in my place," he murmured.

"It looks like that's a new experience for you."

Slowly he smiled at her and shook his head. "I know one other woman who would have chewed me out just like you did. The only difference is, she would have done it in Spanish."

A fierce spasm of jealousy crashed over her. "I see," she said coolly.

He grinned. "I don't think you do. She's a colleague of mine. She's engaged to another man."

Marcus tightened his hand on Jessica's and bent to press a quick kiss to her lips. Had it only been two weeks ago that he was feeling sorry for himself, regretting that she had chosen Carlos over him? Had so much changed in such a small amount of time?

He glanced at Jessica beside him. Apparently it had. He couldn't pinpoint the time when Jessica had become so important to him, but it had happened just the same. She'd crept around the barriers he had erected and found a place inside him.

He saw the uncertain look on her face and cursed his stupidity. Why had he mentioned Margarita? In spite of the way she responded to him, Jessica was a beginner when it came to men. He should have known she'd be hurt and confused.

"She's a good friend, Jessica. Nothing more."

She looked at him, searching his face. "She wasn't always, though, was she?"

How did a twenty-one-year-old become so wise? "It was never more than that on her part," he said ruefully. "I guess I imagined myself in love with her for a while. But I think it was because I knew she wasn't in love with me and never would be. She was safe. I would never have to make a commitment to her."

"Is that so hard for you to do?" she asked softly.

"My only commitment is to my job. That's the way it is, and that's the way it's always been."

"That's a lonely way to live, isn't it?"

"It's the way I've chosen."

He expected her to back away. After all, he had all but told her he wasn't interested in a long-term relationship with a woman. But instead, she let go of his hand and looped her arm through his. "Poor Marcus."

"Poor Marcus? What the hell is that supposed to mean?"

She gave him a serene smile. "I thought we were supposed to be watching what's going on around us. Maybe we should continue this conversation at some other time."

She was right, dammit. He scowled at her, but she was looking around, acting like she wasn't interested in anything but the variety of goods displayed in the stalls. They had reached the market and the crowds milled around the various merchants.

He scowled again, angry with himself. He'd allowed himself to get distracted just when he'd vowed not to let it happen again.

"Give me your hand," he said, his voice cold.

She glanced at him and smiled, ignoring his simmering anger. "I don't see anyone in the crowd paying us any attention. Your partners must be good."

He was startled by her answer. Apparently she'd been watching while he'd been brooding. The thought should have made him angry all over again, but instead he felt a softening in his heart, a feeling of pride in his chest. "It's a good thing one of us has been paying attention," he said gruffly. "Thank you, Jessica."

"I guess we make a good pair." There was a touch of smugness in her voice as she slipped her hand into his.

"I think you've got a smart mouth," he said

mildly. But her words stung his heart. They *did* make a good pair. Not only did they fit together perfectly in bed, but he enjoyed her company just as much out of bed. The dark places in his life didn't seem so dark when Jessica was with him.

And he wasn't going to get used to it. They might have a few more days together, but that was it. It had been a magical two weeks, but outside of the cottage on the beach, there was no place where their lives intersected.

"Let's find some clothes for you," he said, determined not to let his attention be drawn away again. "What do you want?"

They spent the next hour searching through the stalls and tiny shops. Marcus caught sight of Russell Devane several times, as well as two other SPEAR agents he recognized. But there was no sign of the kidnappers.

Finally Jessica turned to him. "I have plenty of clothes now. Is there anything you want?"

Only you. The thought shocked him, and he shook his head quickly. "I wasn't washed up on the shore with only the clothes on my back. I'm fine." He curved his mouth into a smile. "But I'll admit that I'm going to miss seeing you wearing my T-shirts."

She gave him a sultry smile. "I think you might enjoy some of the things I bought even more."

The immediate rush of desire shocked him. "You're teasing me," he muttered, aching with the need to hold her.

"I am, aren't I?" She looked delighted with herself, and he longed to bend down and kiss her. But he merely tightened his grip on her hand. "I've never flirted before. Do you realize that?"

"It sounds to me like you're making up for lost time."

She grinned at him. "I think I like it."

God help him. Jessica was hard enough to resist at the best of times. With a dancing devil in her eye and an exhilarated smile on her face, she was completely beguiling. And she took his breath away. "Let's go find a taxi," he muttered.

Her smile faltered. "Is something wrong?"

"Yeah. We're in far too public a place for what I want to do with you."

Her eyes widened, and he felt her draw in a quick breath. "Oh."

"Yeah. Oh."

He pulled her toward a taxi stand, and they climbed into the first car, a rickety, beat-up vehicle. He hardly noticed the torn upholstery, the musty smell of dampness or the air of neglect. He gave the driver terse directions, then turned to Jessica.

She was staring at him, her eyes huge and dark. He heard her breathing, rapid and shallow in the muffled silence of the cab. He brought her hand to his lips and kissed her fingers, drawing them one by one into his mouth. He felt her shudder when he wrapped his tongue around her pinky, lightly suckling it.

When he released her hand, he bent close to her ear. "That's not what I really want to taste," he whispered. "But you'll have to use your imagination until we get home."

She gripped his hand tightly, and a tiny moan escaped her lips. She was panting, and she blindly turned her face into his neck. He felt her breath on his skin, hot and moist, and then he felt the hesitant touch of her tongue against his neck.

He shuddered and wrapped his arm around her, but he forced himself to keep his eyes open and watch as they drove through the streets of Cascadilla. "Don't," he said in a low voice as she touched him with her tongue again. "I need to pay attention."

"You shouldn't have started it, then."

She was right, he shouldn't have started it. But it was almost impossible not to touch her, not to want her. And he found it terrifying.

"We're almost there," he said. He watched the traffic, looking for anything out of place. But even as he worked, he couldn't let go of her.

After what seemed like an eternity, they drove through the gates of the resort. He gave the driver directions, then leaned back and looked around one more time.

No one had followed their taxi. He was sure of it. They drove past the pool, past the tennis courts, and no one looked out of place. No one watched the taxi, and no one followed their progress through the grounds.

He directed the taxi to stop several cottages before theirs. He fumbled some money into the driver's hand, then stood close to Jessica until the taxi had disappeared. Only then did he turn and take her hand.

They didn't walk directly to the cottage. He pulled her behind a different cottage, and they stood there for a long time as he listened. He wanted to be certain he hadn't led Jessica's kidnappers to her hiding place. As they stood in the heat, his heart raced and his palms tingled, but he knew it wasn't from fear. He wanted Jessica with a desperate hunger, wanted to join their bodies, wanted to shout to the world that she belonged to him.

In short, he wanted all the things he knew he shouldn't have, knew he couldn't have. But that didn't stop the wanting.

She was a physical ache inside him. He wanted to press her against the wall of the cottage and kiss her until she melted into him. He wanted to kiss her until he didn't know where he ended and she began. He wanted to taste every inch of her, explore every bit of her silky skin. He wanted to lose himself in her.

"Is something wrong?" she asked, her voice apprehensive.

He opened his eyes to find her staring at him, anxiety in her eyes. "Everything is fine." *Except my self-control,* he added viciously to himself. "I just wanted to make sure no one had followed us."

And make sure he could keep his hands off her, at least until they got to their cottage.

"Did you see someone behind us on the way back here?"

"No, I didn't see a thing."

Her mouth curved with relief. "You're just being careful. I guess I've never seen you working before. I'll have to get used to it."

"Let's go." He should tell her not to get used to anything about him. It would just make it that much harder for both of them when he had to leave her. But he couldn't force himself to say the words. He had never wanted a woman with such overpowering intensity, such deep-down, all-consuming need. And that frightened the hell out of him.

Chapter 11

As soon as the door to their cottage closed behind them, he pressed her against the wall and fastened his mouth to hers. With a moan deep in her throat, she threw her arms around his neck and pulled him close.

He felt her trembling against him, felt her clutching his shoulders and with a rush of power knew that she wanted him as much as he wanted her. She was as aroused, as needy as he was.

He groaned her name as he kissed her, thrust inside her mouth to taste every bit of her. She opened to him, kissing him back, moving against him so that he thought he would explode.

Suddenly he couldn't bear it for another moment. He had to feel her skin against his, feel the slick slide of their bodies moving together. He reached around and yanked her shirt over her head. He heard the sound of cloth tearing, but he was beyond caring. Frantically he pulled at his shirt, ripping it off, hearing the sound of buttons clattering to the floor. He yanked open her bra and tossed that to the floor, as well.

Her nipples were hard and pebbled, and he groaned as they brushed against the hair on his chest. His fingers trembled as he hooked them into the waistband of her shorts and pulled. Shorts and panties tumbled to the floor, and she stood naked in front of him.

Her eyes were dark and smoky as she reached for him. He felt the shake of her hands as she drew his shorts down his legs, then let her hands trail over him, cupping him intimately. He closed his eyes and shuddered as sensations he'd never felt coursed through him. Power and need expanded inside him until he thought he would explode with the force. His whole being pulsed with the need for her, throbbed with the insistent rhythm of her name.

Her hand tightened around him, and he shuddered convulsively. Groaning, he lifted her and pressed her legs around his waist. Then he plunged inside her, deep into the tight, slick heat he craved.

She gasped his name and dug her fingers into his back. A faraway voice told him to stop, that he was treating her far too roughly. But she moved against him and cried out his name, and he was lost.

He bent his head to take one of her hard nipples into his mouth as he moved against her. She cried out again, tightening her hold on him. He plunged into her again and felt her release clenching around him like a fist. He shuddered once more and poured himself into her.

He stood with his face in her hair, pressing her against the wall, for what seemed like forever. Finally her trembling subsided and he eased her to the floor, rolling her on top of him. Wrapping his arms around her, he held her as tightly as he could.

"I'm sorry," he said when he could speak again. "That was unforgivable."

He felt her raise her head to look at him, but he didn't open his eyes. "What do you mean?" she finally asked. Her voice sounded subdued.

At that he opened his eyes. Her face was still flushed with passion, but he saw the doubt in her eyes. Cursing himself, he stroked his hand down the fall of her hair. "I shouldn't have been so rough, so violent. I should have had more consideration for you. I should have been more careful."

She stared at him for a moment, then her mouth curved into a smile. "Are you telling me that you couldn't control yourself?"

"That's exactly what I'm saying." Anger at what he had done to her blended with burgeoning fear. What was happening to him?

She gave him a sensual smile and curled her hand around his neck, nestling against him once more. "I'm sorry you didn't like it. I thought it was wonderful."

His heart slammed against his chest. "Of course I liked it," he said roughly. "That's not the point."

"Then what is the point?"

"I could have hurt you. I wasn't thinking of your needs."

"I'd say my needs were taken care of quite nicely." She was almost purring.

"Dammit, Jessica, that's not what I mean. I lost control with you. I didn't think, I just felt. And took."

She raised her head, and she was no longer smiling. "I took, too, Marcus. In case you didn't notice, there were two of us making love just now. And nothing happened that I didn't want to happen.''

"How could you know what you want?" The fear had him sitting up, trying to move away from her. "You've never made love with anyone before."

"Is that what's wrong?" she asked softly. "That you're afraid you hurt the inexperienced little virgin?"

He nodded curtly. That was as good an answer as any. He didn't want to talk about what had happened to him on the inside. He didn't want to talk about the fact that he had allowed himself to be totally vulnerable to her.

She gave him a radiant smile and curled into him. "I'd say I went beyond the status of virgin a long time ago. I feel like I've been making love with you for years."

He felt the same way, and it panicked him. The next step would be wanting to continue making love with her forever.

He knew he should move away from her, sever the bonds that seemed to be growing between them right in front of his eyes. But he couldn't do it. Instead, he reached out and pulled her closer. God help him, he couldn't let her go just yet.

"I love the fact that you lost control like that," she murmured. "Can we do it again sometime?"

He groaned into her hair, already feeling himself responding to her. For the past two weeks he had tried to rein himself in, tried to hold back. She was completely inexperienced, and he didn't want to frighten her or hurt her. But after taking her like a rutting animal, she purred against him and told him that she liked it.

"What am I going to do with you?"

He wasn't aware that he'd spoken the words aloud until he felt her smile against his chest. "I have a few suggestions." Her voice was low and sultry, and he felt himself hardening again. She rubbed her leg against his, brushing against his groin. The contact rippled through him like an electric shock. "I never got the chance to model any of my new clothes for you."

"You're not going to need any clothes," he said, rolling her onto her back and fusing his mouth to hers. It was impossible to resist both his desire and hers. "Not for what I have in mind."

She grinned at him, and he saw the devil in her eyes again. "You must be a mind reader. I was hoping you'd say that."

He kissed her again, then swept her into his arms and carried her to the bedroom.

Shadows reached through the windows and touched the bed with fingers of darkness when she woke. Marcus was holding her tightly against him, one of his arms around her. She felt safe and secure and protected.

Just as she had when they made love for the second time. He'd been tender and sweet, loving and gentle. Their lovemaking had gone on for hours. It was as if a dam had broken inside Marcus and his feelings were pouring out.

He would never admit it, she knew. He probably didn't realize that his feelings were reflected in every touch of his hand, every caress, every kiss.

At least she hoped that's what it meant.

She sat up and eased away, staring at him, troubled.

Was he only giving her what he thought she wanted? Was he trying to make up for what had happened earlier?

She couldn't believe that. She had to believe the tenderness and caring had been genuine. And she had to believe that he hadn't realized how much he was showing her.

Because Marcus valued control above all else. She had seen how shaken he was after he lost control. And he would try to regain that control as quickly as possible.

It hadn't happened quickly enough. Her mouth curved as she thought about their lovemaking. Marcus didn't realize how good she was at reading people. It was a skill gained from years of being socially awkward, years of feeling out of place.

And that afternoon she had found all the things that Marcus tried so hard to hide. She hoped he would recognize them for what they were.

"You look awfully thoughtful." His voice, lazy and deep, came through the darkness.

"I was just thinking about what to put in my stomach," she said lightly. If she pushed him, he would run the other way. She knew him well enough to realize that. Marcus wasn't the kind of man who enjoyed talking about his feelings.

The sheets rustled as he sat up and pulled her into the circle of his arm. "I guess I didn't feed you much today, did I?"

"I think we were preoccupied."

"That's one way of saying it." He bent his head and nuzzled her neck, and she shivered. Desire always simmered near the surface when she was close to Marcus. It only took one touch for her to crave more.

He must have felt her response, because his hand tightened on her. Then he sat up. "I guess we should eat."

She laughed. "Don't sound so disappointed."

His eyes gleamed in the darkness. "I'm not disappointed. There's a lot of pleasure to be found in anticipation."

Her blood heated, and she tingled with awareness. "That's what I've heard," she whispered.

"Let's find out." He stood up and pulled her by the hand until she was standing next to him. He seemed completely unaware they were both naked, although she still felt a little self-conscious.

As if he could read her thoughts, he grinned at her. "I've seen it all already, sweetheart," he murmured. "In fact, I think I kissed every inch of your body today." Then he frowned. "No, wait. There's a place I missed." He bent and pressed his lips against the side of her knee, then stood again. "Now I've kissed every inch of your body."

She laughed, her self-consciousness gone, and realized he'd done it on purpose. "I think I have a lot of catching up to do."

His eyes darkened, then he shook his head. "Remember what I said about anticipation? Let's go get something to eat."

She grabbed one of his shirts and headed toward the kitchen, but he stopped her with a hand on her arm. "I have a better idea. Let's go out to eat."

She spun to face him. "Are you sure?"

He shrugged. "As long as we're trying to flush your kidnappers into the open, the more time we spend in public, the better chance we have. You already know that I want to keep you here and safe, but we've agreed that's not going to work. So we might as well flaunt ourselves in public.''

"All right." She remembered the tenseness of their trip to town that morning. "Where do you want to go?"

"Do you have a favorite restaurant on the island?"

"As a matter of fact, I do." She turned to him eagerly. "It's not very big and it's not a tourist spot. But they've got the best seafood on Cascadilla."

"Then that's where we'll go."

"But don't we want to go to the tourist spots?"

"I think we want to do some of both," he said thoughtfully. "Whoever kidnapped you is smarter than the average criminal. They knew enough to lay low for awhile. I would think they would also be smart enough to figure out the kinds of places you like to go." He gave her a grim smile. "I wouldn't be surprised if someone is watching this restaurant if it's your favorite one on the island."

Her joy fizzled like air escaping from a balloon. "And here I thought you wanted to take me someplace special." Her voice sounded petulant, and she wanted to snatch back the words. But it was too late.

He took her hand. "You know I would love to take you someplace special," he said softly. "But right now, your safety is my first concern. And you're not going to be safe until these guys are caught. So we'll go places they'll expect us to go." He lifted her hand and kissed her fingers. "And we can pretend we're on a pleasure trip."

"You're right," she said in a low voice. "I should have thought of that myself."

"Did you buy anything to wear to dinner?"

"I think I could scrounge something up." She

summoned a smile and tried to put the reality out of her head. She might be the bait, but Marcus wouldn't let her be caught.

"Go ahead and get dressed. What's the name of the restaurant? I'll call my partner and warn him we'll be there."

"It's the Blue Goose," she said, walking into the living room to pick up the bags she'd dropped earlier. Marcus had turned away and was dialing the phone. She allowed her gaze to linger on him, on the long, powerful lines of his body, at the fresh scar on his left arm.

He hadn't told her how it happened, only that it was an accident. She was certain his accident was somehow connected to his job. It was a sobering reminder that his job was dangerous and that now she was in danger, too. Turning away, she hurried into the bathroom to take a quick shower.

Twenty minutes later she walked out of the bedroom and came to a halt. Marcus was wearing khaki pants and a dressy shirt. He looked elegant, cool and remote, and she said softly, "Wow."

A faint flush of red stained his cheeks. "I think that's supposed to be my line." His eyes narrowed as he took in her simple black dress. "Are you wearing that in public?"

"What's wrong with this dress?"

"Absolutely nothing." His eyes glittered as his gaze lingered on her, and she had an urge to pull up the low-cut neckline. "But I don't know if I like the idea of anyone else seeing you like that."

"Don't go all caveman on me, Marcus," she said, although his words thrilled her. "This is the style everyone is wearing."

"Believe me, sweetheart, you do things for that dress that no one else could do."

"No one else is going to notice," she said breezily.

"Don't count on it."

She felt the heat in his eyes as he looked at her, and she was exhilarated by her power. Heat washed over her. "Remember what you said earlier about anticipation?"

"I remember," he said grimly. "I'm going to be doing a lot of anticipating tonight. We'll see if it's as much fun as I thought it was."

"We could order room service," she said in a low voice.

But he shook his head. "My partners are in place by now. If we don't show up, they'll think something happened. We have to go."

They walked through the darkened resort, the only lights the faint gas lamps that lined the paths. Marcus took her hand to help her over the rougher parts of the path but didn't let go when they reached the pavement. She could feel the tension that seemed to surround him and knew that not all of it was due to the danger they courted.

She was amazed at herself. She had had no idea she was such a sensual, physical person. Because she'd never had much interest in dating, never wanted to sleep with anyone, she had assumed she was lacking in sexuality. And all the comments she'd heard over the years, all the jeers about her intelligence and her standoffishness, had only reinforced that idea.

But Marcus had completely exploded that idea. And now, after making love with him all afternoon, she couldn't wait to get back to the cottage and make love with him again.

"Scared?" he murmured.

"Not particularly. Why did you ask?"

"Because you're trembling. Are you cold, then?"

The moment of truth was here. Did she tell him the truth and risk scaring him away? Or did she lightly agree that she was cold and preserve the status quo?

"I'm not cold, either," she said.

He turned to look at her.

"I was thinking about you," she said, her gaze steady on his. "And thinking about what we'll do after we get home from dinner."

He sucked in his breath, but he didn't look away. Finally he said, "You know exactly how to make a man uncomfortable, don't you?"

"I didn't mean to embarrass you," she said, laying her hand on his arm.

He snorted. "I wasn't embarrassed. That's not what I meant by uncomfortable."

He looked around and saw they were completely hidden by the surrounding trees. He took her hand and pressed it to his groin, where she had no trouble feeling the hardness of his arousal. "*That's* what I meant by uncomfortable."

"Oh."

"That's something for *you* to think about all evening."

She was still shaking by the time they reached the main building of the resort. Marcus showed her into a cab, then they sat close together while the taxi headed for the center of the island. Neither of them spoke. The air in the cab throbbed with anticipation. She could feel Marcus's body next to hers, hard and tense. He moved his leg, just brushing it against her, and her nerves trembled.

She took a deep breath. If she wanted to concentrate on their surroundings this evening, she had to move away from him.

But she couldn't do it. So instead, she took his hand and began talking. "We always come to the Blue Goose for dinner at least once when I'm home," she said. "It's not very fancy, but the food is good."

His hand tightened on hers. "What's their specialty?"

His voice was too deep, too husky, but he understood what she was doing. She took a breath to settle herself, and turned to smile at him. "Everything."

An hour and a half later she finished her dessert and leaned back in her chair. "What do you think?"

"I think the food was wonderful, and the company was even better."

She grinned at him. "I know a line when I hear one."

"No flies on you, are there?" he said, his lips twitching.

"Not a one," she said, satisfied with the evening. They had managed to talk comfortably about everything and anything, even though Marcus's gaze had smoldered whenever it rested on her. And when he glanced casually around the restaurant every few minutes, she knew he was imprinting all the details on his mind. The open-air design of the restaurant meant they were visible to anyone passing the building. She wondered where his partners were waiting.

"Ready to go?" he said, his casual voice at odds with the fire in his eyes.

"Have we been here long enough?" she asked in a low voice.

"We've been here far too long."

His voice throbbed with intensity. She could hear the desire that pulsed just below the surface, and she felt an answering passion stir inside her. "Then let's go."

He threw some money on the bill that sat on the table, then stood up. He took her elbow to guide her out the door, and she felt the waves of intensity that flowed from him.

As they stood outside the restaurant, waiting for a taxi, she noticed that he used his body to shield hers. "Isn't that defeating the purpose?" she whispered in his ear. "No one can see me."

"I don't want anyone to see you out here," he retorted. "There are too many shadows, too many places to hide. I don't want to worry about a sniper in those trees."

A cold chill washed over her. "I hadn't thought about that."

His face softened as he looked at her. "I don't think it's very likely," he said. "But since those two guys haven't surfaced and we don't know who they are or what they want with you, I don't want to take any chances."

"Did you see anything while we were having dinner?"

"Not much. But I didn't expect to. We were on display tonight. It was up to my partners to watch for your kidnappers."

A taxi pulled up to the restaurant, and they climbed in. She saw Marcus look over his shoulder as they pulled away.

"All clear?" she asked lightly.

He took one more look around, then nodded. "I don't see a thing. But I'm not supposed to. That's my partners' job."

"You trust them completely, don't you?" she asked.

"Yes." He gave a little shrug. "I have to. Because in my business, if you don't trust the people you work with, you're going to be dead before you know it."

His face darkened, and she wondered what he was thinking about. Had he worked with someone who had turned out to be dishonest? Is that how he injured his arm?

"What happened to your arm? I know you told me you had an accident, but did it happen while you were working? Was it because someone was untrustworthy?"

"You could say that."

His low voice burned in the darkness, and she felt his intensity quivering in the air. "What happened to him?"

He found her hand in the darkness of the cab. "Nothing. Yet."

She shivered at the implacable hardness in his voice. Marcus Waters would make a dangerous enemy. "Does he know you're looking for him?"

He turned to look at her, but she couldn't see his eyes in the dim light that filtered through the cab windows. "He knows." She felt him hesitate, as if he wanted to say more, then he looked away.

They rode in silence the rest of the way to the resort. When they finally reached their cabin, he drew her inside without a word.

Chapter 12

"Stay here and don't turn on the lights," he whispered. "I'm going to check a few things."

After searching the cottage for a few minutes, he slipped outside. She heard faint noises around the cottage, the whisper of the bushes that surrounded the small building, a tiny scratching sound against a window.

Marcus reappeared like a ghost, silent and almost invisible. "Is everything okay?" she whispered.

"Fine. I just wanted to make sure there were no signs that the cottage had been disturbed."

"And there weren't?"

"Not one. We should be okay tonight."

She understood what he was saying. They might be safe tonight, but he had no idea how long it would last. Every time they appeared in public, there was a greater chance they would be seen by the kidnappers. And a greater chance of the kidnappers finding their way to the cottage. Just because they were safe tonight was no guarantee they would be safe tomorrow.

He moved silently through the cottage, his dark clothes blending with the shadows until she had to strain to see him. This was his life, she realized. This was what he did. He lived in the darkness, in the shadows of life.

And he made it safer for the rest of them.

Her heart moved in her chest. He took it for granted, but she knew she would have been lost without him. She didn't want to think about what might have happened if Marcus hadn't stumbled across her on that beach.

"Is it all right to turn on the lights?" she asked. She wanted him to come out of the shadows, to stand in the light, at least for tonight.

He took one last look out the window and turned to her. She could see his eyes gleaming without the lights. "Don't bother. We're not going to be in this room long enough to use them."

Her heart began to pound. "Why is that?"

"I have other plans for the night. And they don't include sitting in the living room and talking."

"What do your plans include?" She barely recognized the husky, seductive voice as her own.

"Come over here and I'll show you."

Without taking her gaze from his, she moved a step closer, then another. It felt like she was stepping into an electrical field. The air sizzled around her, and his heat rolled over her in waves, seeking out the places deep inside her.

He stared at her for a moment, then reached out and touched her cheek. His fingers were tentative, almost hesitant. "I've been thinking about this all night,'' he finally said. ''About what I'd do when I got you alone.''

''And what did you decide?''

His blond hair gleamed in the light from a street lamp as he bent his head to trail kisses down her neck. ''I'm going to start by finding out what's beneath this dress.''

She drew in a sharp breath as he moved lower, his mouth burning a trail of heat and need down her chest. ''What do you think I would find here?''

He played with the neckline of the dress, his fingers tugging at the stretchy material, trailing lightly inside to caress her skin. She felt her breasts swell and her nipples harden. ''Why don't you take a look?''

''Not yet.'' He looked at her, and his blue eyes looked black with desire. ''I don't think I want to hurry.''

She wanted to beg him to hurry, to touch her. Every inch of her throbbed with need, pulsated with urgency. But he wouldn't be rushed.

His fingers toyed with the neckline of her dress, brushing over the slope of her breasts, skimming the sensitive skin, dipping into the valley between her breasts. She closed her eyes, wanting only to feel. Then he put his mouth on her breast through the material of her dress, and she moaned his name.

Suddenly he picked her up in his arms and carried her into the bedroom. Stripping off the dress, he looked at her, and his eyes darkened even more.

''Do I take that to mean that you like what I'm wearing?''

His hungry gaze devoured the scraps of black lace she'd found that morning. ''It's a good thing I didn't know what you were wearing under that dress. We would never have made it out of the house.''

She gave him a slow, sexy smile. ''You'll know next time I wear this dress.''

His face tightened even more, and his hands shook as he peeled the lace away. Then he pulled off his clothes and lay beside her.

He made love to her with an intensity, an emotion she'd never felt before. He worshiped every inch of her, kissing and tasting, touching and caressing as if he'd never seen her before.

Or as if he were never going to see her again.

As she clung to him, helpless in the throes of passion, she wrapped her arms more tightly around him as if she would never let him go. And she wondered what he was thinking. Was he afraid their time together was drawing to an end? Was he counting the days, the hours, until he left her?

She wouldn't let it happen, she vowed fiercely to herself. She wouldn't let Marcus leave when her kidnappers had been caught.

But as he pulled her close and she drifted to sleep, she wondered how she was going to stop him.

Marcus woke slowly, reluctantly. Jessica was wrapped around him, her head burrowed against his chest, her hand resting on his thigh. It felt right to hold her like this, frighteningly so. And he knew it was more than time to bring this part of the job to an end.

Gently he disentangled himself and forced himself to move away, to get out of the bed. Jessica had become far too important to him. She was all he could think about. He'd spent more time at the restaurant last night thinking about Jessica, listening to her talk about herself, than he'd spent watching for her kidnappers.

That was dangerous. It was dangerous for her, and it was dangerous for him. Never before had his job come second, and the realization panicked him. It was time for him to get the hell out of Cascadilla.

It was time to catch Simon, he corrected himself coldly. That was the point of everything he'd done since he'd been here. That was the point of trying to catch Jessica's kidnappers. He was sure they would lead him to the traitor.

Only if Marcus did his job would Jessica be safe. And his job involved dragging her around the island, using her as bait.

It was a hell of a job, he thought savagely. He stormed into the kitchen to make coffee, his emotions in a knot and confusion blackening his mood. His need to protect her, to keep her cocooned in safety in this cottage warred with his need to catch Simon. And he lost, no matter which one he chose.

"Good morning," Jessica said behind him, her voice sleepy and content.

He didn't turn to face her. "I figured you'd sleep later than this."

"I woke up when you got out of bed. I couldn't sleep without you next to me."

The flash of joy took him by surprise. He allowed it to swell inside him for a moment before he deliberately squashed it. He couldn't afford that kind of hope. "Seems like you've done it for the past twenty-one years," he said in what he hoped was a casual voice.

She came up behind him and wrapped her arms

around his waist, and he couldn't stop himself from leaning into her. "That's before I knew what I was missing."

He bent and kissed her, savoring her taste. Then he eased himself away. "How about some breakfast?"

Out of the corner of his eye he saw her grin. "I don't know why, but I'm hungry all the time lately. I guess I'm just more active than I have been."

"I guess so." Her gentle teasing stirred his blood, and he wanted to turn and take her in his arms, carry her back to bed. Instead he moved away. "I guess I better give you some food, then. No telling what you'll do if I don't feed you."

"I can see you don't want to take any chances."

She leaned against the counter, her eyes laughing at him, and all he wanted was to bury himself in her, to lose himself in Jessica until nothing else mattered.

But something else did matter. Simon mattered, he reminded himself grimly as he began to prepare breakfast. And he'd better not forget it.

"What's the plan for today?" she asked, her voice completely trusting.

He couldn't afford to respond to that trust. "I thought you might like to go snorkeling."

She jumped away from the counter, her face blazing with pleasure. "Really? You think it's safe?"

He shrugged. "As safe as anything else. We want to be seen around the island, and that's as good a way as any." He felt his heart soften as he looked at her and saw how excited she was. "And I knew it was something you'd enjoy."

"Thank you, Marcus." Her eyes shone. "I can't wait to show you our reefs."

"Are there places where we can stay fairly close

to shore? I don't want to get too far out in a boat. We'll be far too vulnerable and isolated.''

She nodded slowly. "We won't be able to see the best reefs, but we can see enough." She grinned at him, her eyes bright. "I can take you to the best reefs later, after we don't have to worry about the kidnappers."

There would be no later for them. He would be gone as soon as Simon was caught, as far from Cascadilla as he could get. But he couldn't bring himself to say that to her. He didn't want to wipe that excitement out of her eyes, that happiness from her face.

"Let's eat, then." His voice was too abrupt, but he didn't think she noticed. She was too excited about snorkeling. "Then you can tell me where we're going so I can let my partners know."

"I'll make up a list."

She slid into one of the kitchen chairs and grabbed a piece of paper. After thinking for a moment, she began writing.

While they were eating, she gave his questions only perfunctory answers. She was too absorbed in what she was doing. In spite of his warnings to himself to back away from Jessica, he was fascinated. He imagined this was how she would act when she was working.

No wonder it had been so easy for those two men to grab her, he thought. She wouldn't have heard a thing until they were on top of her. He suspected that a parade could have gone by outside the window and she wouldn't have noticed.

She was a lot like him that way.

The thought shocked him, then made him uneasy. But he had to acknowledge the truth in it. While she was working, she was totally absorbed in what she was doing. Just like he was.

No wonder she understood him so easily.

The thought crept, unbidden, into his mind. He tried to banish it, but it stubbornly refused to leave. Other than Margarita, a fellow agent, he had never met anyone who understood his intensity about his job, understood his commitment to it. Even Heather, so many years ago, hadn't understood. And he thought he had loved Heather.

There was no comparison between Jessica and Heather, he thought, panic rising. They were as unlike as two people could be.

Then why was he comparing Jessica to Heather? Why was he assuming that Jessica would have the same reaction to his job as Heather had?

It wasn't just his job. He and Jessica came from different worlds. And she was far too young for him.

But the pat answers didn't feel right anymore. They didn't fall as glibly from his tongue. Jessica might be years younger than he was, but she was his equal in every way that counted.

He was veering far too close to forbidden waters, he told himself, and he stood to clear the table. He would be doing Jessica a grave injustice if he tried to hold on to her. She belonged in her own world, a world that didn't deal in death and fear and destruction. She deserved to live in a world without shadows, a world full of people like herself.

And totally unlike him.

"Ready to go?" He glanced at her and was rewarded with another blinding smile.

"Just about. How long do you want to be gone? And do you want to go to more than one beach?"

"That would be best, I think." He forced himself to concentrate on the problem of the kidnappers. Mooning about Jessica wasn't going to get them caught.

"Good." She beamed at him. "That's what I was hoping you would say. I've picked out four places to try."

"Sounds good." He reached for her list. "Let me call my partners."

She handed him the piece of paper and leaned back in her chair. "They must be good at what they do. Other than the time I saw one of them step out of the alley, I haven't seen them at all."

"You're not supposed to see them. And neither are the kidnappers. With any luck, those two won't see our men until we've slapped the handcuffs on them."

Some of the smile left her eyes. "Do you think that will be soon?"

"I have no idea. So far, they've played this exactly right. They've stayed out of sight, they haven't talked and they haven't tried to snatch anyone else, at least as far as we know. But if they're still around and still looking for you, we'll get a hit sooner or later."

"Do you think they're still around?"

He hesitated for a fraction of a second. "We have to assume they are." If Simon was involved, Marcus could almost guarantee it. The traitor had gone to too much trouble to give up so easily.

Apparently she didn't notice his hesitation, because she nodded. "All right, then, let's give them some opportunities to find us."

He picked up the phone, called Devane and told him their plans for the day, then read the list of beaches where they could be found. Then he hung up and turned to Jessica.

"Are these all beaches where you've snorkeled in the past? Are they places someone who knew you would look for you to go snorkeling?"

She nodded. "I usually go to the reefs that surround the island, the ones you can only access by boat. They're more suitable for my research. But if I'm going to snorkel from the shore, these are the ones I would choose."

"And people would know that."

Her eyes darkened. "Are you implying that someone would have sold me to those men? That someone would have told them how to get to me?"

"They had to get the information from somewhere," he said gently. "It doesn't mean someone deliberately betrayed you. The information could have been gleaned in an innocent conversation. The person who gave away the information might not have even realized what he did."

Her eyes were troubled. "I hope so."

He ached when he saw how he'd shattered her trust. He'd do anything to give it back to her, he realized. But once broken, it couldn't be fixed. *Welcome to my world,* he thought grimly.

It was only another illustration of how bad he would be for her, how wrong it would be to drag her into the darkness with him. Jessica would only be disillusioned if she stayed with him. Above all, he didn't want to see her become as cynical and hard as he was.

"Can we pick up the equipment we'll need somewhere in town?" he asked to distract her.

She nodded, then her eyes brightened. "If they're

smart, those kidnappers would be watching the dive shops. They'd know I didn't have any equipment with me and that I'd need it.''

"Good thinking. Where are we going?" He waited for her answer, then pulled out the phone and called Devane again. "Put someone on Boss Frog's Dive Shop. We'll be stopping there for equipment. Jessica suggested they may be watching the shops.''

He closed the phone and leaned over to kiss her. "I hope you don't turn to a life of crime," he said lightly. "We'd be hard-pressed to keep up with you.''

"Don't worry about that," she said, equally lightly. "I much prefer working with you. I don't think I'd like to be your enemy.''

She'd never be that. Emotion stirred inside him again, and he tried to ignore it. Emotion had no place in this job. He needed to catch Simon, and that was all he could focus on.

It was all he could afford to focus on. Because if he didn't, he'd begin to make mistakes. And this time, the stakes would be too high to contemplate.

"Ready to go?" he asked.

"All set." She jumped up from the table, her eyes shining with anticipation. "I can't wait.''

They caught a taxi again, and Jessica leaned forward to give the driver directions to the dive shop. When the taxi slowed, Marcus looked around with narrowed eyes.

He didn't like this neighborhood. The dive shop was a tiny storefront, tucked into a maze of small shops and buildings. Most of the shops had apartments over them, the perfect locations from which to watch the shop and not be seen. There was too much traffic; there were too many alleys and too many side-walk cafés.

"Do we have to stop at this shop?" he asked in a low voice.

She snapped her head around to look at him. "What's wrong?"

"Nothing, yet. But there are far too many places for someone to hide. If the kidnappers are watching for you and they're as smart as we think they are, my men might not ever see them."

"John, the owner of the shop, taught me to dive, and I've never gone anywhere else," she said, staring at the shop with an almost wistful look in her eyes. Marcus felt a black wave of jealousy wash over him. "But I suppose we could try another shop."

"No, we'll go to this one." He leaned forward to pay the driver. "Hell, it's what we want, isn't it?" He opened the door with a savage twist of his hand. "We want them to spot us. I just have to count on my partners being good enough, and lucky enough, to spot the kidnappers."

"Right." She gave him a bright look, but he could see that her eyes were troubled. "Let's go inside."

"No, stand here for a moment." His gut clenched at the thought of making her a target, but that was why they'd come. "Are you sure this is where some-one would think you'd go?"

"Absolutely. Everyone knows that John taught me to dive. I always visit him when I'm home, and we usually go diving together."

"So you'd be expected to go to this shop." He ignored his surging jealousy.

"Yes."

"Fine," he said, his voice more curt than he liked.

"Then let's go inside. We've given them enough of a chance to see you."

She gave him a sidelong glance but didn't say anything as they walked into the shop. A curtain of beads hung in a doorway behind the counter, and he heard the tinny sound of a doorbell ringing in the back of the store. A moment later the beads rustled and a man appeared from the back.

He was thin and wiry, his face like tanned leather. His gray hair hung down his back in a thin braid. When he saw Jessica, his eyes lit up.

"Jess! I didn't know you were coming in. Why didn't you call?"

"This was a spur of the moment decision," she said easily. "John, this is Marcus, a friend of mine. I want to show him the sights and I don't have my equipment with me. Can you fix us up?"

"You bet." John's eyes were on him, assessing. "You want to scuba?"

"No, we're going to snorkel. But I want the best you have."

He turned to Jessica. "That's all I'd give you, sweetheart."

The man's eyes softened, and he stepped close to give her a hug. Marcus's hands itched to push him away, but he clenched them into fists and pretended to examine the masks hanging from a rack by the door.

"You don't want those," John said, misinterpreting his interest. "I'll get equipment for you from the back."

He disappeared behind the beads again, and Marcus looked at Jessica. "You seem very chummy."

He couldn't keep the sourness from his voice, and she looked at him with surprise. "What's wrong?"

I'm a stupid fool, he thought bitterly. *That's what's wrong.* "Nothing. I guess I'm anxious to get out of this shop." That was the truth. For more than one reason.

"This won't take long."

She was right. They were out of the shop ten minutes later, after Jessica asked John to put their rentals on her bill. She gave him another hug that had Marcus grinding his teeth, then they emerged into the sunlight, carrying their equipment in mesh bags.

Marcus looked around casually, letting his gaze catalog everything he saw. Nothing appeared out of place, but his neck burned as if he was being watched.

He pretended to drop his bag, and as he bent to pick it up, he looked behind him. As he straightened, he made a complete circle on the sidewalk.

He didn't see anyone who took an unusual interest in them, no one who stared at them. He couldn't see Devane or any of the other agents. But he knew they were there. He trusted them with his life. He hoped to God they saw whoever was watching them.

"What's wrong?" Jessica asked in a low voice.

"I don't know. But someone is watching us."

Her face paled. "The kidnappers?"

"I'm not sure."

"I hope so," she said fiercely.

"My partners are here, too," he reminded her. "If someone follows us, they'll know."

"Good." She tucked her arm in his and gave him a wobbly smile. "Then we can forget about them and think about where we should go first."

She was amazing. The men who had kidnapped her

might be close by, watching them, but she managed to smile and act as if nothing was wrong.

''You're something else,'' he muttered. He couldn't help himself. He covered her hand with his and squeezed.

Her face relaxed, and she turned her hand to join with his. ''I think that's my line. Are you ready to go snorkeling?''

Chapter 13

Jessica sat in the taxi and watched Marcus. His head moved constantly, watching out the windows, checking behind them. He'd worn a grim and determined look on his face since they'd walked into the dive shop, and his mood had steadily blackened since.

"Are you all right?" she finally asked.

He turned to look at her. His eyes were as hard and cold as stones. "Why didn't you tell me you had a personal relationship with John? We would have kept that shop staked out from the very beginning."

"What do you mean, a personal relationship?"

"You're obviously close friends." His voice was stiff.

"Because I hugged him?" She stared at him, amazed. Then she saw the uncertainty deep in his eyes, and warmth uncurled inside her as she understood. Marcus was jealous of John.

"John is one of my oldest friends," she said gently.

"I've known him and his wife since I was ten. He taught me to dive and shared all his favorite spots with me. But that's all there is."

"It doesn't matter what your relationship is, just that there was one." His face was still hard, but some of the warmth came back into his eyes. "You don't owe me any explanations."

"Maybe I don't owe you an explanation, but I want to give you one. John is a good friend, nothing more. And he never will be more."

He searched her face for a long moment, then finally sighed. "I'm being a jerk, aren't I?"

"Yep. But I think I like it." She smiled at him and reached over to kiss him. He tucked her hand into his arm and resumed looking out the window. But his face was no longer shuttered and remote.

"Have you seen anyone following us?"

"Not a soul. And traffic is thinning out enough that I would. Maybe I was wrong. Maybe no one was watching at the dive shop."

"But you don't think you were wrong, do you?" she asked quietly.

He shrugged. "I usually trust my instincts. They've saved my rear end enough times that I pay attention. But nothing about this case is usual. So I don't know."

"Your partners were watching, weren't they?"

"I'm sure they were, although I didn't see them."

"So if anyone tries to follow us, they'll spot them."

"I hope so."

But she could see he was still worried. "Do you want to do this another day?" she asked.

"No. This is why we're here. We want to draw

them out. We'll go to the four places that you picked and hope that my partner and his men spot them somewhere along the way.''

''All right.''

He leaned against the upholstery and gave her a smile. ''And besides, I'm afraid you would kill me if I changed my mind about snorkeling now.''

''I wouldn't kill you,'' she said, giving him a grin. ''But I might have to hurt you a little.''

His eyes gleamed. ''That sounds very…interesting.''

Before she could answer, the taxi stopped at the first beach. She flung open the door and jumped out as Marcus scrambled after her. They put their clothes in a locker, and Jessica led the way to the water, already pulling on her mask and breathing tube. Since Marcus had dived before today, he didn't need any instructions. When they both had their fins on, she turned to him.

''I usually just walk out until the water is about waist deep, then I start swimming. We're heading over there.'' She pointed to a large rock that jutted into the water off a small point. ''That's where the reef is. But you can usually begin to see fish before we get there.''

''You lead and I'll follow you,'' Marcus said, taking one more look over his shoulder in the direction of the road. She understood. He didn't want her to ever be out of his sight. He would stick close by in the water.

She gave him a thumbs-up, then turned and waded into the water. It was pleasantly cool, and she grinned as it washed over her skin. She couldn't wait to show Marcus the splendors of a tropical coral reef.

When the water lapped at her waist, she launched herself into its silky embrace. Immediately she saw schools of tiny, silvery fish darting back and forth in front of her. She waited until she felt Marcus next to her, then began to swim in the direction of the rock.

This was a reef for the tourists, and therefore a good place to start. It was close to the shore and easily accessible, and all the tourists eventually snorkeled here. It was a logical place for her to take Marcus.

She hoped the kidnappers would think so, too.

The dark wall of the reef loomed ahead of her, and she surfaced and blew water out of her tube. Marcus immediately surfaced next to her. "What's wrong?"

"Nothing. I just wanted to orient you. We're going to have to swim around that rock. The more interesting part of the reef is on the other side, where it's more protected. Be careful because the water gets pretty shallow. Try not to put your hands on any of the coral, or scrape your knees. It can be really sharp."

"Got it." He looked around, and she followed his gaze. There were a few other people snorkeling close by, but they'd all been here before she and Marcus arrived. "Looks like we're okay."

She nodded and slipped her breathing tube into her mouth, then went underwater. She made her way around the rock, knowing exactly how far she had to go. Larger fish darted past, among them a small school of queen angelfish with their dramatic black-and-white-striped bodies. A group of blue tang in the water ahead of her looked almost iridescent. Finally she turned the corner and emerged into the brilliant world of the coral reef.

Jessica glanced behind her and saw Marcus on her

heels. He gave her a thumbs-up sign when he saw her looking at him, and she smiled. Even underwater, Marcus looked like he was keeping watch.

The reef undulated in front of them, the water so shallow that it felt like she could reach out and touch the coral. Clumps of brain coral, its surface deeply ridged, hid starfish and sea anemones. Fish darted everywhere, their brilliant colors an underwater rainbow.

She turned in the water to watch Marcus. He floated on the surface, staring down at the strange, twisted formations of coral, and Jessica smiled again. The reef had entranced even Marcus.

After a while he looked at her, and she could see the wonder on his face. He gestured toward the deeper water, and she followed him to the surface.

"It's incredible! I've never seen anything like it."

"You never saw a reef while you were training for scuba diving?"

His mouth thinned. "We weren't on sight-seeing expeditions. Gawking at the beauty under the water wasn't on our agenda."

"You can make up for it today."

"I wish," he began, then he stopped abruptly. But she saw the flicker in his eyes and knew what he wanted to say.

"I wish we could just concentrate on looking at the reefs, too," she said quietly. "I never get tired of it."

"It doesn't matter what we want to do," he said, his voice strained. "We came out here for a reason. How long do you think we should stay before we move to the next beach? What would be reasonable for a beginner like me?"

"Even in this warm water, you're going to get

chilled if you snorkel for more than forty-five minutes without taking a break," she said. "So maybe we should quit after a half hour and go to the next place."

"Sounds good. I'll keep track of the time."

She smiled. "You know me too well already. I usually set an alarm for myself so I know when to get out of the water. But I don't have my dive watch."

"I'll let you know when we need to move on."

They swam for another twenty minutes. She pointed out the various animals that inhabited the reef, promising with sign language that she would explain later what they were. Finally Marcus tapped his watch, signaling that it was time to swim toward the beach.

A stingray swimming along the sandy bottom of the lagoon a little way from the reef caught his attention, and he stopped to watch it. The ray glided along the sand, his powerful fins undulating, stirring up the sand in his search for food. Jessica swam a little farther, then waited for Marcus.

He looked up and saw she was ahead of him, then pulled next to her with a few powerful strokes. They swam until their feet touched the bottom, then they stood and pulled off their masks.

"Thank you," he said quietly. "That was wonderful."

But he seemed more remote, more withdrawn. His gaze swept over the beach, cataloging the tourists, looking for anyone out of place. They floated in the water for a long time, letting the waves carry them closer to shore.

Finally he said, "I don't see anything that looks suspicious. Let's go."

They retrieved their clothes from the locker and began looking for a taxi. They dried quickly in the hot tropical sun, and by the time they found a cab, Jessica's bathing suit was almost dry.

They visited two more beaches, each time watching carefully before slipping into the water. They never saw any sign of the kidnappers, or of Marcus's partners.

Finally, as they were walking into the water at the fourth and last beach, Jessica said, ''I can't believe they haven't been watching these beaches, especially if they saw me at the dive shop. These are the only logical places to go on the island if you don't have a boat.''

''We don't know what's happening on the beach,'' he said, glancing over his shoulder as they waded deeper. ''My partner may have seen them or even caught them.''

Jessica was shocked at her gut reaction. She didn't want the kidnappers to have been captured yet. She wasn't ready to say goodbye to Marcus.

''Maybe so,'' she managed to say.

Marcus gave her a sharp look, but he didn't say anything. They were heading to a reef that was offshore, but close enough to swim to. ''Ready?'' he asked.

''Let's go.''

The water slid over them like warm satin, and she gave herself up to its sensuality. A school of small cornet fish glided past, their long, thin bodies looking like silver sticks. She could see the shadow of the reef far ahead of them. Suddenly a dark shape appeared below them.

She saw Marcus's instinctive start, and he moved

closer to her. Then she smiled. It was a large sea turtle, moving through the water just above the sandy bottom of the lagoon.

Both she and Marcus turned to follow the turtle. He swam steadily, occasionally slowing to browse through a clump of turtle grass for food. Sea turtles looked ungainly and awkward on land, but in the sea they were magnificent. Marcus appeared as entranced as she was.

Finally Marcus tapped his watch, and they surfaced. "We've been in the water for almost an hour," he said.

"I guess I lost track of time," she answered.

"So did I. We'd better get back."

She started to turn toward shore when Marcus put his hand on her arm. "Wait."

She turned to face him, but he was looking toward the open sea. There was a small boat bobbing on the waves not too far away. Two men with binoculars peered toward the beach.

"Does that boat look familiar?" he asked quietly.

Her stomach clenched as she studied the boat. "It does," she said slowly. "But then, it looks like most of the boats around here."

"I can't get a good view of their faces. Do you think that's the pair that grabbed you?"

She stared at the boat until it wavered in front of her eyes. "I'm not sure," she finally said. "It could be. But why are they out there instead of on the beach? How will they be able to find out where we go?"

"They must have someone else on the beach," he said, his voice grim and hard. "Someone you can't identify. They're a lot smarter than I gave them credit for. And I already thought they were pretty smart for petty criminals.''

"What do you think it means?" She tried hard to hold on to her self-control. But the sight of the boat, which looked very similar to the one in which she'd been kidnapped, was making her shiver with fear.

"I think it means we need to get out of the water and pay close attention when we're on our way home."

Immediately she turned and began swimming for the beach.

Marcus watched her for a moment, then turned and followed her, cursing himself as he swam. Simon must be close by. It was the only possible explanation. He'd sent his henchmen out on a boat to watch for Jessica, where no one could identify them or arrest them. He'd stayed behind to follow Jessica home, knowing she couldn't identify him.

And Marcus wasn't sure if he'd seen enough of Simon in the confusion in Madrileño to identify him, either. He'd caught a glimpse of the traitor, but in the mud and confusion and gunfire, it had only given him a brief impression of Simon.

His smooth, steady strokes would have carried him to shore much more quickly than Jessica, and he slowed to wait for her. She was tired, although he knew she would never admit it. He'd seen her moving more slowly through the water, paddling harder to float on top.

As soon as his feet touched bottom he stood and ripped off his mask. There was no sign of anyone watching the water with more than a casual interest, no sign of anyone waiting for them.

But Devane and his men were good enough, and careful enough, that he wouldn't see them.

And he was afraid Simon was, too.

Cursing under his breath, he practically dragged Jessica onto the sand. She looked at him, and he could see the alarm in her face.

"What's wrong?" she asked, panting. "Do you see someone waiting for us?"

"Not yet," he answered without looking at her. But he suspected that Simon was close by. He studied the bushes and trees that lined the beach, looking for movement, for light glinting off a weapon or binoculars.

He didn't see a thing.

"What do we do?" Jessica asked in a small voice.

"Exactly what we planned to do." He headed toward the place where they'd concealed their belongings, still not taking his eyes off the vegetation.

Was that a movement to the right? He froze, then started to run in that direction. But he stopped almost immediately.

He couldn't leave Jessica alone. And he didn't have his weapon. It was hidden in his clothing. Grinding his teeth with frustration, he ran over to his clothes, throwing them over his wet swim trunks. He shoved his gun into the waistband and pulled his shirt on to cover it.

But when he looked at the clump of bushes again, he knew it was too late. Whoever had hidden there was gone. He could feel it. There was no energy humming from that place, no smell of fear and excitement. His prey had vanished.

So close! Simon might have been just out of reach,

only yards away from him. And he'd been forced to let him go.

And maybe that was exactly what Simon had wanted him to think, he told himself. As soon as he'd headed toward the trees, someone could have jumped out and grabbed Jessica.

With a last look behind him, he slung an arm over Jessica's shoulder and steered her toward the road. "Let's catch a taxi and head home."

"What about the men on the boat?" she asked.

"I can't do anything about them. But if Dev—my partner is here, and he should be, he'll have seen them."

"So we're going to lead them to us." He felt her shiver in the heat.

"That's the idea. That's what we hope to do." He tightened his grip on her. "But don't worry, Jessica. I'll be with you the whole time. Nothing is going to happen to you."

She looked at him, surprised. "I know that. I'm worried about you and your partners."

A wave of some emotion he didn't want to think about or name rushed over him. "Don't," he said gruffly. "I can take care of myself."

"I know you can. But that doesn't mean I won't worry." She reached up and touched the scar on his arm. "I suspect you thought you could take care of yourself when that happened, too."

"That's not important." The only thing that was important was catching Simon. And protecting Jessica. "Let's go." He heard the hard, implacable tones of his voice and glanced at Jessica. Apparently she hadn't noticed.

Or she had noticed and understood.

Unease prickled on his skin, and it had nothing to do with Simon. Why did it feel as if there was an unbreakable connection binding him and Jessica together? And why did it feel as if it was pulling tighter every day?

It was only natural, he told himself. It was the danger, the threat. The adrenaline.

But it was more than that, and he shied away from examining it more closely. It was time to finish this job and move on. Maybe then he wouldn't be plagued by this restlessness, this need for more.

He'd never needed more before. His job had always been enough. Never before had he felt this vague dissatisfaction, this unexplained yearning.

It was this damned island, he told himself. The pace was too slow and the weather too perfect. It was the kind of place where a man could lose himself, lose sight of what was important. It was the kind of place where a man could get caught up in sensuality and lose track of his priorities.

It wasn't about to happen to him. With any luck at all, Simon would be behind bars before the end of the week. And this time, Marcus vowed, the traitor would stay behind bars.

They found a taxi and climbed inside. As they drove home, Marcus watched out the rear window. There was a lot of traffic on this part of Cascadilla, and cars were constantly entering or leaving the stream of traffic. But he didn't see any one car consistently behind them.

"Is anyone following us?"

"I'm not sure," he answered, reluctant to take his eyes off the scene behind him. "I haven't seen one car in particular, but no one said it was going to be easy.''

''What do we do?''

''The same thing we've been doing. We go back to the resort. And then we wait.''

Jessica slipped her hand into his. ''Just tell me what to do.''

Finally he turned to look at her. ''You continue to amaze me, Jessica.''

She cocked her head and gave him a puzzled look. ''What does that mean?''

''It means that very few people I know, men or women, would have sat there calmly and asked what to do. Most people would have panicked.''

She gave him a smug smile. ''I guess most people don't know you, then. I know you won't let anything happen to me. I just want to help you catch these two men so we can get on with our lives.''

And that was the crux of the matter, he suddenly realized. He wasn't sure he wanted to get on with his life. He wanted to stay in this paradise, in this cottage, with Jessica. Forever.

That was never going to happen. As much as they enjoyed each other's company, as much as he wanted her, she wasn't for him. Everything he'd learned about her proved it. Today had just been the punctuation mark.

''What are you thinking?'' she murmured, slipping her hand into his.

''I'm thinking that your world is about as far away from mine as a person can get.'' And that wouldn't change, no matter how much he wanted it to.

''I don't think that's true,'' she protested.

''Look at what we did today.'' His voice was ruthless. "You live in a world of beauty, a peaceful, tranquil world. My world is guns and fighting and ugliness. I sure don't see any place where those worlds connect."

"I think they connected today," she said softly. "You enjoyed the snorkeling, didn't you?"

"You know I did."

"I can bring a little beauty and peace into your world."

"And what can I bring to yours?" He refused to look at her.

After a single beat, she said, "Excitement."

He heard the laughter in her voice and looked at her with astonishment. "How can you even joke about this, Jessica?"

"I'm not joking about it. But don't you see? My world is far too staid and calm. Far too orderly. I need someone like you, someone who can shake things up, show me different things, different perspectives. We fit perfectly together."

He knew what she was saying, and it scared him to death. He deliberately chose to misunderstand. "Sex isn't everything in a relationship."

"I wasn't talking about sex."

"What else has there been between us?"

She was silent for a moment. Then she said quietly, "I think we've shared a lot about ourselves. I feel like I know you, Marcus. And I know you know me better than anyone else. Including my family."

"Then all I can say is you've led a sheltered life."

"My point exactly," she said, triumph in her voice. "And in the last few weeks I've discovered I don't like it."

"Well, with any luck, you're going back to your

sheltered life real soon. Sooner or later your kidnappers will figure out where we are. And then we'll have them.''

He glanced behind him again and saw a car that looked familiar. It had moved into the line of traffic soon after they'd left the beach, but turned off the road after only a short time. "In fact, this may be our man right now.''

She started to turn to look, but he held her still. "No, don't look. I don't want him to know I've seen him.''

The taxi pulled into the resort, and the car kept going along the road. The driver kept his face turned away as he passed the taxi, then speeded up.

In a few minutes they were in the cottage. Marcus locked the doors carefully, then looked at Jessica. "Now, we wait.''

Chapter 14

Marcus paced the cottage most of the afternoon, checking the locks and bolts, cleaning his weapon, staring out the windows. Finally the phone rang, and he grabbed it and stepped out the door. He didn't want Jessica to overhear him.

"What did you find?" he asked.

"Not a thing. It was the two kidnappers in the boat at the last beach. We got a good look at them, but they vanished. I don't know where they docked the boat."

"What about on the beach? Did you find anyone?"

"No." Marcus could hear the frustration in Russell Devane's voice. "He was well-hidden, and we realized too late that he was there. Whoever it was, he was damned smart. He paid a bunch of kids to create a diversion, then he slipped away."

"It was Simon," Marcus said grimly. "Bet on it. Those two punks who grabbed her aren't smart enough to put this together. I can see his fingerprints on this whole operation.''

''What do you want us to do now?''

''Watch this cottage. I'm sure we were followed back to the resort. Sooner or later, they'll make a move, and I'm betting on sooner. Simon has to be getting desperate for money.''

''Will do.''

Marcus closed the phone and went inside. He found Jessica sitting on the couch, watching him with huge eyes.

''My partner is sure those were your kidnappers in the boat,'' he said, sitting next to her. ''But they didn't find anyone on the beach.''

Jessica watched him for a moment. Then she said, ''But you think someone was there.''

''I'm sure of it.'' The certainty twisted in his gut. He had been so close to Simon!

''And now we wait around for the kidnappers to try and take me back.''

He took her hand. ''That's the plan. But if it scares you too much, I can get you to a safe house. Then I'll wait here for them myself.''

Slowly she shook her head. ''You can't be sure they're not already watching us. And if I leave, they'll just follow me there. I'd rather stay here, with you.'' She watched him steadily. ''I trust you, Marcus. I know you won't let them take me or let me get hurt.''

The weight of responsibility pressed on his chest like a stone. He'd been responsible for people before. But never someone he'd cared so much about. Her trust was frightening.

''Are you sure?''

''Of course I am.'' She reached out and touched

his arm, and his whole body responded. "I'd rather be here with you than anywhere else. Even knowing that the bad guys are coming."

"My partners are going to be watching the cottage. With any luck, they'll catch the kidnappers before they even get to the place."

"I know." She smiled and touched him again, and he couldn't resist putting his hand over hers. He needed physical contact with her, even if it was only a fleeting caress. "I guess this means an evening swim is out of the question."

He stared at her in disbelief, then realized that she was grinning at him, her eyes twinkling mischievously. "Some people might think you weren't taking this very seriously," he growled.

Her smile faded. "I'm taking it very seriously. But I don't want to sit here worrying for the next few days."

"Then let's see what we can do to occupy ourselves." He saw the hot flash in her eyes and shook his head. "I need to concentrate. And if we made love, I sure wouldn't be concentrating on anything but you."

"All right." But the disappointment in her eyes made his heart leap with joy.

He stood and opened one of the cabinets under the bookcase. "There are a bunch of games in here. How about if we play one?"

She gave him a doubtful look. "Are you sure you want to play games? That doesn't sound like you."

"It's not what I would normally choose," he admitted. "But I can't think of any other way to pass the time."

"All right." She moved to stand next to him. "How about we play that game of trivia?"

"Fine by me."

An hour later he stared at her with mixed disbelief and humor. "You didn't tell me you were a trivia expert. I believe that's the third time you've kicked my butt."

"I guess you're lucky we didn't make bets on the outcome, aren't you?" she answered, her voice smug.

He narrowed his eyes. "That's it for this game. Now I get to choose."

He pulled out a game of strategy and conquest and proceeded to annihilate her. When he took the last of her armies, she flopped back onto the couch with a grin.

"I guess you showed me," she said.

He had the grace to look embarrassed. "I guess I don't handle losing real well."

"Now why does that not surprise me?" she said with a laugh.

He paused as he put the game away and looked at her. "You're not angry?"

"Why would I be angry? I did the same thing to you with the first game." She leaned forward, the smile fading from her mouth. "And you wouldn't be the person you are, couldn't do the kind of work you do, if you liked to lose. So we'll just call it even."

"You continue to surprise me," he said, sitting back and watching her, that uncomfortable yearning seizing him again.

"What do you mean?"

"How do you understand so much about me?" he asked in a low voice. "How is it that you seem to know just what I'm going to do?"

She watched him for a while, and tenderness crept into her eyes. He wanted to dive into it, and the need to do so made him ease away from her. Finally she sighed. "For a smart man, Marcus, you can be pretty dense sometimes. Let's just say that I've had plenty of opportunities to study you."

He didn't want to follow this conversational path, he realized. It was skating far too close to feelings he didn't want to think about. "How did you get to be such an expert on trivia?"

Her mouth curled into a smile. "It's real easy when you don't have a life. I spend most of my time reading, both for my research and for pleasure. It's amazing how much information you pick up that way."

"No wonder you graduated from college so early."

"You know just as much, Marcus," she said gently. "You just know different things than I do."

He didn't want it to be true. He wanted to emphasize the differences between them, maintain the facade that he was far too different from her for them to be compatible. But with her watching him out of her huge amber-colored eyes, he was forced to nod. "Maybe so. But the things I know aren't going to win me any prizes."

"They'll save my life," she said. "I think that's a little more important."

"Yeah, well, it depends whose side you're on, I guess." He deliberately tried to steer their conversation in a lighter direction.

"I guess it does," she murmured.

He couldn't tell what she was thinking, and it made him nervous. "You about ready for bed?" he asked.

"I think so." She stood and stretched. "I didn't

think I would be able to sleep tonight. But I'm exhausted.''

Heat speared through him as he looked at her, the long, elegant lines of her body silhouetted in the dim light. But he tamped it down, then buried it deep inside. He couldn't afford to let himself be distracted tonight. He expected the kidnappers to pay a visit to the cottage later.

''Go on to bed, then. I'm going to stay up for a while.''

''You expect them tonight, don't you?''

He could lie and tell her no, that he wanted to read for a while. But she deserved the truth. ''I think so. They don't have anything to gain by waiting.''

''All right.'' She nodded. ''Good night, Marcus.''

''Good night,'' he murmured, watching her disappear through the door to the bedroom. He listened to the rustle of her clothes as she undressed, listened to the sound of her moving around in the other room and longed to join her. He wanted nothing more than to lie down beside her, to fit her body against his and lose himself in her.

But he turned away and went to stand by the window. The night sky shimmered with stars, and the moon hung low on the horizon, bathing the ground with pearly light. Simon was somewhere on Cascadilla, and with any luck, they'd take the first step toward capturing him tonight. That was the only thing he could afford to think about.

He stood by the window until he could no longer hear Jessica in the bedroom. When he'd heard nothing but silence for a long time, he moved to the couch and turned out all the lights in the room.

Slowly his eyes grew accustomed to the darkness,

and his other senses sharpened. He heard the night birds calling from the trees outside, heard the whisper of the surf as it crept onto the beach, then rolled out to sea. He smelled the flowers that the resort planted everywhere, sweet and mysterious. Far in the distance, he heard the low murmur of evening at the resort, the voices of people on vacation, dedicated to pleasure.

He wasn't here on vacation.

Deadly serious business would be conducted here tonight. Simon would be a fool if he didn't try to recapture Jessica tonight, before they had a chance to set up their defenses. And Simon was no fool.

Neither am I, Marcus thought grimly. Devane and two other agents would be in place soon, waiting close by for the kidnappers to approach. They'd agreed that the kidnappers would probably wait until early morning, when there was less chance of being discovered.

Marcus stretched out to wait, letting his mind wander. It wanted to wander in Jessica's direction, but he tried to put her out of his mind. He would have to give her up soon, and he didn't want to think about that. It was going to hurt too damn much.

A tiny voice said he didn't have to give her up. Jessica didn't want him to go. He could read that in her eyes every time she looked at him.

And God knew he didn't want to leave her. But it was the only right thing to do. She deserved a chance to make a good life for herself. And waiting at home while he chased the bad guys all over the world wasn't the kind of life he wanted for her.

He wanted nothing but the best for Jessica. She deserved someone who would always be there for her, someone who was there every day, who came home every night. Someone who could give her all the things he couldn't, like stability and security.

He jumped to his feet, irritated. He didn't want to think about Jessica with anyone else. He couldn't bear the thought of someone else holding her, someone else kissing her. He scowled. He didn't want to think about anyone but himself touching her.

"So think about something else," he growled. He moved to the window, listening. Nothing moved outside but the wind.

He paced the tiny living room, but it didn't help. Finally he sat, thinking about the opportunities SPEAR had had recently to catch Simon. The traitor had slipped through the net every time.

Not this time, he vowed.

A tiny sound outside the cottage caught his attention, and he froze. Then he heard it again. It was the sound of a small pebble rolling along the sand. And it came from the back of the cottage.

Was one of the other guests taking a midnight swim? He strained to listen, but the sound wasn't repeated. Anyone with innocent reasons for being on the beach would make more noise than that. Silently he moved to the door of the cottage. Devane and his men would be out there. They'd make sure no one got into the cottage and got to Jessica.

He waited until he heard the sound again. It was closer this time. It sounded like it came from behind the next cottage. He moved silently to the door and put his hand on the doorknob. He'd let the intruder get a little closer, then he'd open the door and give the signal to Devane and the others. They were in the trees at the front of the cottage. There was no cover for them to hide on the side of the cottage facing the beach.

He heard Jessica move in the bedroom, and he froze. Then there was silence, and he began to breathe again. *Come on,* he told the intruder silently. *Just a little closer and we'll have you.*

But he didn't hear another footstep. Whoever was out there was being very cautious. And it was no less than he expected. Simon wouldn't make their job easy. SPEAR had already found that out.

Finally he heard it again, another tiny sound. His hand closed around the doorknob and he turned it, ready to pull the door open and leap outside. Then he heard Jessica again.

She cried out in her sleep, sobbing with fear. He heard his name, and he instinctively moved into the cottage.

"Get away from me," she sobbed. "Marcus? Marcus, where are you? Help me!"

She was dreaming, he realized immediately. Knowing that the kidnappers might try to capture her again tonight, she'd fallen asleep and dreamed of just that. She wasn't in any real danger. He could leave her and she wouldn't know the difference.

But he couldn't force himself to walk out the door and leave her suffering. He couldn't ignore the sounds of her pain. So he opened the door and signaled to Devane, gesturing toward the back of the cottage. Then he went inside and hurried to Jessica's side.

"It's all right, sweetheart," he murmured, sliding onto the bed next to her. "I'm right here, and nothing is going to happen to you."

He wrapped his arms around her, and she gripped him tightly. "Wake up, Jessica. You're dreaming."

He kissed her cheek and brushed her hair out of her eyes. "Wake up, sweetheart."

Groggily she opened her eyes. He saw her struggle to focus, saw the moment she realized he was with her. "Marcus?"

"You were having a dream," he said, holding her shoulders as he kept his gaze on her face. He wanted her to see him, to know that he was real and not part of her dream. "But it's okay. I'm here and you're all right."

"I dreamed they caught me again," she said haltingly. "And I didn't know where you were." She searched his face. "Am I awake now?"

He lowered his mouth and kissed her, and felt her softening against him. "Does that feel real?" he murmured.

"Mmm." Her low sound of pleasure hummed in his blood, and he leaned closer. Then he heard the sound of running feet pounding past the cottage, and he jerked his head up.

She came fully awake and sat up in bed, clutching the sheet. "What was that?"

"I think it might have been what we've been waiting for."

"Go," she said in a low voice. "I'm awake and I'm fine."

He looked at her, still reluctant to leave. And then he stood slowly. He felt as if the world had suddenly tilted, throwing him off balance. He'd chosen to stay with Jessica rather than try to catch Simon.

Simon had been the focus of his job, of his life, for the past eight months. And when faced with a choice, he'd chosen Jessica.

His priority had always been his job. He'd never hesitated to put it first, never wanted to do otherwise.

And all that had changed in the past three weeks.

Since he'd met Jessica.

"Why are you staring at me?"

"Am I?"

She nodded. "You look odd, Marcus. Are you all right?"

No, he wasn't all right. He didn't think he'd ever be all right again. "I'm fine," he said hoarsely. "I'm going to step outside and see what happened. Are you sure you'll be okay by yourself?"

"Positive. Go."

He turned, his head spinning, his heart pounding in his chest. What the hell was wrong with him?

"I'm fine," she repeated in a low voice. "Go ahead."

She thought he was reluctant to leave her alone. God, if she only knew what had been going through his mind. But he pushed himself out of the bedroom and hurried to the door of the cottage.

By the time he'd reached the beach, he saw Devane standing at the edge of the water, his weapon drawn. The moonlight illuminated the frustration on his face.

"What happened?"

"Someone was here, all right," Russell Devane said, his voice tight with anger. "The clever bastard jumped into the water when he heard us coming." He nodded toward the horizon. "There's a raft waiting for him out there."

Marcus saw a dark object bobbing low in the water, too far out to be seen clearly. "What was he planning to do? Make her swim out to the raft?"

"He probably had someone with a car close by. The others are checking it out."

Marcus watched as the raft tipped and a dark figure slipped over the edge. Then they heard the faint sound of an outboard motor, and the raft headed out to sea.

"I'll be damned," Marcus said softly.

"We all will be." Devane thinned his lips. "We have to catch that slimy bastard, Waters. Before he does any more damage to SPEAR."

"We still have Jessica. And this proves that Simon still needs money. He'll try again. And we'll have him next time."

"I'm counting on it." Devane jerked his head toward the cabin. "How's she holding up?"

"She's doing just fine. Anxious to catch these guys."

"What do we do now?" Devane asked, turning away from the beach. The raft was out of sight.

"We wait. It may not be tomorrow night or the night after that, but they'll come back. And next time we'll have them."

"Let's go see what my men found." Devane's mouth tightened again. "But I'm betting they found squat."

Jessica glanced out the window and saw Marcus standing with another man on the beach. She heard the low murmur of their voices, and even from a distance she could hear the frustration and anger. Clearly, the kidnappers had gotten away.

It didn't matter. She was safe with Marcus, and they would have another chance.

And she would have more time with Marcus. More time to make him see that what they had was unique and wonderful.

She turned from the window and started a pot of coffee. She suspected that neither of them were going to get much more sleep tonight.

A few minutes later the door to the cottage opened and Marcus came in, accompanied by one of the men she'd met when she'd helped draw the picture of the kidnappers. He nodded to her, his eyes stormy.

"What happened?" she asked Marcus.

"There was someone here. But he got away. Dove into the water as soon as he heard Devane." He jerked his head in the other man's direction. "He swam out to a raft. We suspect there was a car waiting somewhere close by in case he was successful."

She wondered if Marcus realized he had identified his partner, something he had been careful not to do. "What do we do now?"

"We wait," Marcus said grimly. "They'll be back. The fact that they tried to grab you tonight means they need the ransom money badly."

There was more going on than a foiled kidnapping. Jessica was sure of it. Her gaze went from Marcus's closed, tight face to the anger burning in Devane's eyes. There was far more going on here. But she'd wait and ask Marcus about it later, when they were alone.

"I put some coffee on. I figured you wouldn't be sleeping tonight."

She saw Devane and Marcus exchange a glance. Marcus shrugged. "Might as well stay here for a while. They probably won't be back tonight."

There was a knock at the door. Marcus's hand hovered over his gun as he looked out the window, then he pulled open the door.

Two men stood there. When Marcus looked at

them, they shook their heads. "Gone. There was a car parked between two cottages a few doors down. We heard it leaving before we reached it. We looked around for any evidence they might have left behind, but we didn't see a thing."

"Check it out in the morning," Marcus said, and the two men nodded.

"I'm going back to bed," Jessica announced. It was clear that her presence was inhibiting the men from talking.

Marcus looked at her. "Will you be all right?"

She summoned a tired smile. "With the amount of firepower in this cottage right now, I should sleep like a baby."

His face softened. "Good night," he murmured.

His voice was a caress, and she wanted to reach out and touch him. Instead, she nodded and turned away. As she closed the door to the bedroom, she heard the men's voices, the words muffled and unclear but the tone urgent and angry.

Chapter 15

The next three days passed agonizingly slowly. Jessica watched as Marcus paced the cottage. They didn't go outdoors. They ordered their meals from room service. And when Jessica questioned the wisdom of revealing her presence, Marcus shook his head. "It doesn't matter now," he'd said. "They already know you're here."

They read the books on the bookshelves, but she couldn't concentrate on the words. They talked, but Marcus was uncommunicative, answering her questions in short phrases and not offering any conversation. Finally, on the third night, Jessica said, "I need to go to bed." She needed to get away from the unrelenting tension that swirled through the cottage.

"Go ahead," he said absently. "I'm waiting to hear from Devane."

She wanted to question him about Devane, and about himself. Clearly Marcus knew more about her kidnapping than he had told her. But she told herself to wait until after the kidnappers were caught, when she would have his undivided attention. She didn't intend to let Marcus brush her off with partial answers or placate her with half-truths.

"Good night," she said softly.

He turned to look at her, and his face softened. For an instant he was the Marcus she had fallen in love with. "I'm sorry this has turned out this way," he said in a low voice.

"It hasn't turned out any way yet," she retorted. "But I know you're going to catch them."

He leaned forward and kissed her. "You're good for my ego," he said, running his finger down her cheek. "But I don't walk on water, you know."

She gave him a tired smile. "I know that. If you did, you would have caught the guy the other night. But you're close enough."

He smiled at her, kissed her again, then straightened. She realized it was as much as she was going to get from him. "I'll see you in the morning," she said.

He nodded absently, already looking out the window. "I'll be here."

She closed the door behind her and got ready for bed. She knew Devane would be here shortly, and they would want to talk. And she didn't want to eavesdrop on them.

The sheets were crisp and cool, but the bed felt too large and too empty. She wanted Marcus beside her, wanted to wrap her arms around him and lose herself in him. He had been pulling away from her the past three days, distancing himself, as if he was already preparing to leave her.

She didn't intend to let that happen. She wanted to make Marcus see that they belonged together, that they could make a life together. But she was afraid he was going to be stubborn.

She smiled as she cuddled Marcus's pillow to her chest. He didn't know how stubborn she could be when she was determined. And she was determined to make Marcus see that they fit together perfectly.

She heard the front door open, and as she drifted off to sleep she heard the low murmur of voices from the other room. It was surprisingly reassuring. Marcus would protect her. She was safe.

Marcus watched Russell Devane walk in the door to the cottage and felt a deep pang of regret that he wasn't with Jessica in the bedroom. But that was the way it had to be.

"Are your men in place?" he asked quietly as Devane closed the door.

"They have been for several hours now. I don't want to take any chances this time."

"I thought we would stay in the house from now on, let him get inside the next time he shows up. It'll be a lot easier to grab him in here."

Devane looked toward the closed bedroom door. "She doesn't mind?"

"I haven't told her." His voice softened. "But she would tell me to do what we needed to do."

"She's okay," Devane said gruffly.

She was more than okay, Marcus thought. But he couldn't afford to think about Jessica right now. He had to be focused completely on what might happen here tonight.

"You all set?" he asked the other agent.

When Devane nodded, Marcus said, "Then I'm going to turn off the lights. We'll sit and wait for them."

They sat in the darkness for hours. The noise from the resort gradually faded until the only sounds were the night birds and the surf breaking over the beach. The moon slowly set until it shed only a vague hint of light low on the horizon. And still there was no sound from beyond the cottage.

Finally, close to three o'clock, Marcus heard the sound he'd been waiting for. It was only a whisper, the careless scrape of a shoe against the sand. But it brought him out of his chair. Devane moved at the same time.

Soundlessly they took their places on either side of the door. Marcus glanced at his fellow agent, and Devane nodded. The men waiting in the trees outside wouldn't interrupt. They would allow the intruder to enter the cottage unchallenged. No one wanted a repeat of the other night, when the kidnapper had fled into the water and out of reach.

Endless minutes passed. Marcus strained to listen, but didn't hear any other sounds. Either the kidnapper was being remarkably careful or something had spooked him and he'd changed his mind.

He wasn't about to gamble Jessica's life on that possibility, he thought as he shifted and tightened his grip on his gun. He intended to stay by the door until the sun was up and people were moving around the resort.

Another movement came from outside, this one no more than a change in the flow of air through the window. Someone had stepped in front of the cottage.

Marcus looked at Devane, who nodded. He'd felt it, too. Both men melted farther into the shadows.

Marcus took deep breaths, visualizing what would happen when the intruder entered the cottage. He would be on the floor, with two guns at his head, before he knew what had happened.

The boards on the porch creaked slightly, and Marcus tensed. When the doorknob began to turn, he gathered himself, preparing his muscles. The intruder would not escape this time.

A thin slice of light appeared at the door, barely brighter than the inside of the cottage. Marcus rolled forward on the balls of his feet, ready to spring. The door opened wider, and a figure all in black slipped into the room.

Marcus sent the door crashing shut as he and Devane leaped for the intruder. Simultaneously, their guns were cocked and pointed at his head.

"Down on the floor," Marcus growled. "Spread your arms and legs. And do it now."

The figure froze, and Marcus tensed. Was he going to try to fight? Then the figure collapsed on the floor, stretching out his arms and legs.

"Please don't hurt me," he quavered.

Marcus dropped to the floor and pulled out handcuffs, fastening them around the intruder's wrists and placing another pair around his ankles. Then he rolled him over. It was the young man who had worked on Jessica's father's island. He recognized him from the picture the police artist had drawn. Devane kept his gun steadily trained on the intruder's head. The door to the cottage opened again, and the men who had been hiding in the trees moved silently inside.

"Look what we have here," Marcus said quietly as he searched the man. He pulled a nasty-looking blackjack out of his pocket, followed by a knife. "Looks like our boy didn't want to make any noise."

"That's too bad," said Devane.

"Yeah." Marcus sat on his heels and gave their captive a stony stare. "Because he's going to be making lots of noise in a few minutes."

Just as he'd hoped, the kidnapper's eyes filled with fear. "What are you going to do to me?" he sobbed.

He was hardly more than a boy, and Marcus knew they'd have his story in a matter of minutes.

"That depends on what you make us do." He leaned closer. "My partner and I are reasonable. If you tell us what we want to know, there's no reason anyone has to get hurt tonight."

He left the implication hanging in the air and watched the young man's face turn a greenish color.

"I'll tell you anything you want to know," he gasped.

"Not very loyal to your employers, are you?"

"It doesn't matter," he muttered. "I'm not going to get paid now."

"What are you doing here?" Marcus snapped.

"Trying to get the girl back. She's worth a lot of money."

"To whom?"

"To Simon."

Marcus exchanged a triumphant look with Devane, but schooled his face to be expressionless when he looked at the boy on the floor. "What's your name?"

"Tommy. Tommy Kalendar."

"And who's Simon?"

"He's the guy who hired us to kidnap the Burke girl."

Marcus frowned. "You and who else?"

"Steve Trace. He needed me to get onto the Burkes' island," Tommy said proudly. "I used to work there and I knew how the security system worked."

Marcus heard the bedroom door open, but he didn't look up. Jessica deserved to hear what had happened. "So it was this Steve Trace's idea to kidnap Jessica Burke?"

Tommy shook his head. "It was Simon's idea. But Simon hired Steve, and Steve hired me."

"And how were you supposed to contact this Simon after you kidnapped the girl?"

Tommy shrugged. "I don't know. That was Steve's job. He's the only one who talked to Simon. I just followed orders and did what I was told."

"And what was the plan for tonight?"

"I was going to knock the girl out and carry her to a car that's waiting. I lift a lot of weights," he said, giving his captors a cocky smile. "That would have been easy for me."

Marcus didn't ask how he'd intended to incapacitate Jessica's protector. Clearly this kid hadn't thought beyond the money he would receive. Instead, he said, "And then what?"

"Then Steve would have called Simon, we'd have gotten our money, and Simon would have taken over."

"All right," Marcus said. "Where were you going to take the woman?"

He heard Jessica move, but he kept his gaze focused on the boy's face. Tommy's eyes dropped. "I don't know if I can tell you that. From everything Steve has said, Simon won't be happy if I tell you."

"We won't be happy if you don't." Marcus leaned

toward him menacingly. "And we're the ones with the power right now. And the weapons."

Tommy shrank back as Marcus casually fingered the knife he'd found on the boy. "Steve is in an apartment in town. He's waiting for me."

"Where?"

Tommy hesitated, and Marcus laid the knife, blade down, on his chest. Tommy gulped and blurted out an address. Jessica gasped, and Marcus looked at her. "What is it?"

"That's right across the street from Boss Frog's Dive Shop," she whispered.

"I'm not surprised. Simon is damned smart."

"Who is Simon?" Jessica asked, her voice quiet. But when he looked at her, Marcus saw the hurt in her eyes.

"I'll tell you later," he said. "Everything."

Devane glanced at him sharply, but Marcus ignored him and kept his gaze on Jessica. Finally she nodded. "All right."

Was it as simple as that? He had been deceiving her for the past three weeks, and with one nod of her head, she had forgiven him. Barely able to believe her generosity, he felt his heart contract painfully in his chest. He wanted to go to her, to fold her in his arms and ask her to forgive him, but he wrenched his attention to Tommy.

"You're going to go with these men, Tommy. They have lots of questions for you." He leaned closer and looked deep into Tommy's eyes. "And if we find that you've lied to us, I'm not going to be happy at all. And I think you know what that means."

"I haven't lied," Tommy said shrilly. "Steve is waiting for me there."

"He'd better be."

Marcus instructed one of the men to stay with Jessica, and the other took charge of Tommy. He would be interrogated by SPEAR, but Marcus was afraid there was little more the boy could tell them. Simon was notorious for insulating himself from the people he employed.

"Let's go," Marcus said to Devane.

The two men headed for the door. At the last minute, Marcus turned to look at Jessica. "I'll be back soon," he murmured.

She gave him a tiny smile. "I know."

Her two words lifted his spirits and lightened his heart. She was amazing. Instead of being angry with him for not telling her the truth, she was telling him that she trusted him. He raised his arm in a silent salute before he slipped out the door.

Marcus and Russell Devane drove fast through the streets of Cascadilla, desperate to find Steve Trace before he could escape or warn Simon that the gig was up. They parked two blocks from the dive shop and ran through the silent, deserted streets until they were several buildings away from the apartment. It was on the third floor of the building, and they quickly split up. Marcus headed up the front stairs, and Devane took the rear.

But when they kicked in the door to the apartment, they found it deserted. Trace had apparently left in a hurry. A bottle of beer was still on the table, cold and sweating. There was a bag of chips, half-eaten, next to it.

"How did he get out of here so quickly?" Devane asked.

Marcus gestured toward the open window. "My

guess is that he had some kind of alarm rigged. When we tripped it, he took off.''

He walked to the window and saw a rope hanging to the ground. ''The oldest trick in the book,'' he said, disgusted with himself.

Steve Trace stood on the corner of the street and watched one of the men in his apartment look out the window. ''Outsmarted you, didn't I?'' he snarled. He didn't bother to watch any longer, but turned and hurried away. He'd taken the precaution of parking his car far away from the apartment. At least he had transportation.

And he could contact the boss, Trace thought. Warn him what had happened. Simon still owed him and Tommy their money. And since these two had found the apartment, it was a safe bet that Tommy wasn't going to be asking for his money any time soon. Trace smiled as he walked quickly toward the market area. It looked like payday was going to come twice.

He found a pay phone and dropped in some coins, dialing the number he'd memorized. Simon answered after one ring.

''Do you have her?''

''There was a problem. I think they have Tommy.''

Waves of anger sizzled through the phone line. ''That's unfortunate,'' Simon finally said. ''But I suppose there's nothing to be done about it now.''

''What about our money?''

''Your money?'' Simon laughed, and the sound chilled Trace's blood. ''There's no money for you. You didn't succeed in kidnapping the girl. Without the girl, there is no ransom money. And without the ransom, you don't get paid.''

''What about everything we did?''

''It was most appreciated. But you didn't do what I needed you to do. You showed a lot of promise, Trace. Unfortunately, you weren't wise in your choice of associates. Be more careful in the future. It's too bad I'm not staying in this part of the world. I could use someone like you.''

The phone clicked, and Trace heard nothing but the dial tone. Slowly he put the phone into its cradle, rage churning his blood and turning his vision red.

It was all that bitch's fault. He swore viciously as he hurried toward his car. She's the one who wrecked things for them. If she hadn't jumped out of the boat, he'd have his money by now. And he'd have a regular job with Simon, and the possibility of a lot more money.

It was all her fault. And he was going to make her pay.

Marcus closed the door behind Devane and the other SPEAR agent, then took a deep breath and turned to face her. He'd asked his partner to give him time alone with Jessica. She'd barely said a word since he and Devane returned to the cottage.

''Is it really over?'' she said quietly.

''Not yet. But it shouldn't be long before we catch Trace. We contacted the Cascadilla Police Department and they're looking for him, too. He can't go far on an island.''

''And what about Simon?'' Her voice was barely above a whisper.

''I'm sorry, Jessica. I owe you an explanation.''

"You don't owe me anything, Marcus. You did what you promised to do. You protected me from the kidnappers, and you caught one of them."

Her steady voice made him shrivel inside. He would have preferred her to yell at him, to accuse him of lying to her. Her quiet words tore his heart out.

"I lied to you."

She gave him a cool look. "I imagine that's not unusual in your line of work. You're not really in law enforcement, are you?"

"Not in the way I've implied. Are you angry?"

Slowly she shook her head. "I'm disappointed, but you did it to protect me. How can I be angry with you for that?"

Her generosity of spirit shamed him. He was used to trusting no one. And Jessica trusted him completely. "I'm not used to telling anyone what I do," he muttered.

Surprisingly, she smiled. "I already figured that out. But don't worry, your secret is safe with me."

And he knew it would be. Jessica would never betray him. He would never have to watch his back when he was with her.

But he wasn't going to be with her for very much longer, he reminded himself harshly. Just long enough to clear up the loose ends in this case and get her safely to her parents.

He didn't want to think about that right now. He looked at her, sitting on the couch, her feet tucked under her, wearing one of his shirts, and he felt his resolve melting.

Surely they could have one more night together, one more chance to make memories that would have to last a lifetime. He took a step closer to her. "Can I tell you everything in the morning? I don't really want to talk right now."

Her eyes darkened, and he saw her body tense beneath his shirt. "What did you have in mind?"

He reached down and pulled her off the couch. She leaned into him, and he smoothed his hand down her back. She fit against him perfectly, as if she were made for him. "I've neglected you the past few days."

He bent and kissed her neck, and felt the shudder that rippled through her. "I've missed you, Marcus."

"Can it really be that easy for you to forgive me?" he asked, nuzzling her throat.

"Why don't we find out?"

She leaned her head back to look at him, and what he saw in her face made him catch his breath. She glowed at him, the warm honey of her eyes giving him a message he didn't want to hear. The truth beat against his heart, demanding to be admitted. But fear fluttered inside him, too, and he closed his eyes.

"Don't look at me like that," he groaned.

"How is that?"

"Like you think I hang the moon."

She laughed, and the sound rippled over him like liquid silk. "You're not perfect, Marcus. Far from it. But you're what I want."

She meant right now, he told himself, panic stirring. She wasn't talking about anything more than this moment, more than this night.

She couldn't be. Because he was determined to do the right thing. And that meant taking her to her parents and walking away.

"I need you, Marcus."

Her whispered words surrounded him, drew him into a web of desire he was helpless to avoid. Groaning, he bent to taste her mouth. As she melted against him, he tightened his arms around her. For just this night, he could pretend he never had to let her go.

For just this night, she could be his.

While it was dark outside, he could allow his hidden dreams full rein. While the night embraced them, he could delude himself into thinking they were real. Because they were as shadowy as smoke and would vanish as readily in the light of day.

She wrapped her arms around him and tried to draw him closer. Heat speared through him, and he swung her into his arms to carry her into the bedroom. Before he could move, he heard footsteps running outside the cottage.

Instinctively he set Jessica behind him and reached for his gun. He had set it on the kitchen table. Before he could lunge for it, the door to the cottage crashed open, and a man lunged into the room.

Chapter 16

Jessica flinched and reached out for Marcus. But he set her behind him and stepped forward to face the intruder. The man's brown hair was tousled, and his eyes were wild with hatred. "Get away from the bitch," he growled, pulling a gun out of his pocket.

Marcus reached back and lightly pushed her toward the bedroom door. "Who are you?" he asked. His voice was calm and even.

"She was mine," the man shouted. "I caught her, and I was supposed to get the money. Now he's gone and it's all her fault."

"Who's gone?" Marcus asked. Jessica saw his body tense as the other man came closer. She shivered as she saw the stranger's eyes. They glittered with blood lust and rage, and the fury they shot at Marcus told her the intruder was completely beyond reason.

"Simon." The other man spat the word. "Simon's gone. And he didn't pay me the money he owed me."

"Why was that?" Again, Marcus's voice was level and calm, but the other man's face darkened.

"He didn't get any ransom money. So he didn't pay me." He stared at Jessica, and hatred contorted his face. "It's her fault. And she's going to pay."

"You must be Steve Trace," Marcus said.

"What difference does it make?" The man sneered.

"I like to know who I'm talking to."

"It doesn't matter. We won't be talking for long."

Marcus fluttered his hands toward her, and she realized that he wanted her to move into the bedroom. Slowly she took a step backward, watching the man with the gun. As she moved, Trace took a step closer. "There's no place to hide in there, bitch," he growled. "You're only postponing it."

Marcus motioned for her to move again. Clearly he had a plan, and she slowly took another step. "I thought you were smarter than this, Trace," Marcus said. "Why aren't you as far from Cascadilla as you can get?"

"I had some unfinished business." His head swiveled toward Jessica, and he instinctively took another step closer. "Once I take care of her, then I can leave."

"Not so fast." Marcus kicked suddenly, and the gun went flying from Trace's hand. Trace stared at it dumbly for a moment, and Marcus jumped on him.

The two men wrestled on the floor, the cottage silent except for their grunts and curses. There should be more noise, Jessica thought as a bubble of hysteria filled her chest. One of these men was going to die, and there was no noise.

And it was up to her to make sure it wasn't Marcus.

She tried to get to the gun, but it had slid under the couch, and the two men were in the way. Her gaze darted around the room. She spotted Marcus's gun on the kitchen table.

She ran to grab the gun. As she was spinning back to the living room, she saw a knife they'd used to cut a pineapple. She grabbed that, too, and ran into the living room.

She saw Marcus looking at her out of the corner of his eye. "Knife," he gasped, and she set the gun carefully out of reach on the floor. She waited until Marcus stuck out his hand, then she slapped the knife into his palm.

The blade flashed in the light as Marcus whipped it toward Trace's throat. "Freeze, you bastard," Marcus growled. "Or it'll be the last move you make."

Trace lunged again, but the knife pricked his throat, drawing blood. "Don't make me kill you, Trace," Marcus said very quietly. "Don't make me do it."

Trace stilled, and Marcus shifted so he squatted on the floor next to him, the knife held firmly against the intruder's throat. "You're going to answer some questions for me, Trace."

"Make me." Trace sneered.

With a flick of his wrist, Marcus drew the knife along his cheek. Blood welled in bright red beads. Jessica felt her stomach roll, but Trace was apparently convinced that Marcus was serious. He lay perfectly still on the floor. "What do you want to know?" he finally asked, his voice sullen.

"When did Simon hire you?"

"About a month ago."

"How did he find you?"

"It's not hard to find the right man for the job if

you know where to look," he snarled. "And I have connections."

"I bet you do," Marcus muttered. "How did you find Tommy?"

"Simon had a list of Burke's former employees. I started at the top and worked my way down to Tommy."

"And why did you pick Ms. Burke?"

Their captive's eyes flashed. "Because her father could pay the ransom money."

"Who did you think Simon was?"

The man on the floor shrugged. "Someone who needed money. Or maybe someone with a grudge against Burke. I didn't care. The only thing I cared about was the money."

"And where is Simon now?"

"How the hell should I know? He said he was leaving the area." Rage twisted his face again. "He said he could have used a man like me. I could have been working for him, and now he's gone."

Marcus tensed, and Jessica saw him shift closer to Trace. "This is important, Trace, so pay attention. And you'd better answer me straight. A knife can do a lot of damage to a man before it kills him. When did he say he was leaving?"

"Tonight. I called him."

"From the phone in your apartment?"

"I called him from a phone in the market after I left the apartment."

"Which phone?"

"How the hell should I remember that?"

"Try real hard," Marcus said, grabbing Trace's hair and pulling back his head. He laid the blade of the knife against Trace's throat. "Because to tell you the truth, I'm getting tired of you."

For the first time, Jessica saw real fear in Trace's eyes. He stuttered out an address, and she quickly wrote it down. Marcus glanced at her and gave her a quick glance of approval. "Now call and tell Devane to get over here," he said to her, and gave her the number.

Before she could move to the telephone, Trace jerked away from Marcus and lunged at her, ignoring the cut the knife left on his throat.

Marcus leaped on his back and wrapped his arms around his neck. Trace ignored him, still trying to reach her. His face was contorted with hatred, and his eyes were almost black with rage.

"Stop, Trace," Marcus panted. "I don't want to kill you."

But the man was beyond reason. He struggled and Jessica could see it took all of Marcus's strength to hold him. Finally, Trace made one mad lunge for her, and a loud crack echoed through the cottage.

Trace's eyes widened suddenly, then he went limp. Marcus eased his body to the floor, then dropped the knife and stepped over to Jessica.

"I'm sorry, sweetheart. Sorry you had to see that." He wrapped his arms around her.

She burrowed into the comfort of his embrace, shaking almost uncontrollably. "I was afraid he was going to hurt you."

"It wasn't me he wanted," Marcus said grimly. "He wanted to kill you."

"Shouldn't we tie him up?" she asked.

"He's dead." Marcus's voice was flat. "His neck is broken."

She shuddered. "Are you sure?"

"I'm sure." He reached around her to pick up the phone and dialed a number. After a moment, he said, "Get back over here. And bring damage control."

He drew her into the other room and positioned himself so he was in front of her. "I didn't have a choice," he said in a low voice. "I could see he was beyond reason and determined to kill you. And I would have died myself before I let him touch you."

"I know." She reached out and touched his cheek. "Thank you," she murmured. "You saved my life."

He wrapped his arms around her, dragging her against him. She could feel him trembling. "I can't ever remember being that scared," he whispered against her hair. "Are you sure you're all right?"

"I'm fine. He never touched me. You made sure of that."

He pulled away and looked at her, touching her face, smoothing his hand over her hair. It was almost as if he needed to reassure himself that she was still alive. "God, Jessica, I'm sorry you got dragged into this mess."

She held him tightly as she thought of the dead man in the other room and couldn't stop the shudder that rippled through her. But then she looked at Marcus and saw the pain in his eyes. Pain for her, she realized. And she had to tell him the truth. "Parts of it were awful," she said frankly, "but I'm not sorry it happened. If I hadn't been kidnapped, I never would have met you."

"That's a hell of a thing to say."

"It's the truth. The awful parts are over. And I still have you."

His eyes cooled, and she saw regret mixed with

determination. To stop him from saying the words she didn't want to hear, she pulled his head down and kissed him. He stood rigidly for a moment, as if he was trying to stop himself from responding, then groaned and pulled her closer.

She had no idea how long they stood there in the kitchen, holding one another. She lost herself in the emotions that bubbled through her, the relief and love and joy. She lost herself in Marcus.

Suddenly he straightened and moved away from her. He headed for the front of the cottage, and she heard the sound of running feet.

The door burst open, and Russell Devane ran into the room, followed by three other men. They all froze when they saw Steve Trace's body on the floor.

"What the hell happened?" Devane said in a cold, deadly voice.

"It's Trace. He wanted Jessica. So he came to get her."

"And you had to kill him?"

"Yes."

Jessica heard the implacable, emotionless tone of his voice and shivered.

"But he told us what we need to know before he died."

Quickly he repeated what Trace had told them, including the information about the phone call to Simon. "Get to that phone and get the number, then find out who he called. There aren't going to be many other calls from that phone at this time of night. We still have a chance to grab the bastard."

"I'll do that." Devane turned to the other three men. "You take care of the body. The usual procedures."

"Call me as soon as you have anything," Marcus said.

Devane nodded. "Will do." He ran out the door and disappeared into the darkness.

In a matter of minutes the three men had removed Steve Trace's body and disappeared, as well. Jessica stared at the room, disoriented. It looked exactly as it had just an hour ago. There was no trace of the violent death she had witnessed.

"It's okay," Marcus murmured. "We can move to a different cottage."

"No," she said, transferring her gaze to Marcus's face. Resolve hardened inside her. "We don't have to move. But I do want some answers."

He nodded. "Fair enough. I'll tell you everything I can tell you."

He sat at the kitchen table, and she sat across from him. Almost absently, he reached out and took her hand, and she curled her fingers around his.

"I work for a government agency," he began, then he hesitated.

"Are you a spy?" she asked, her eyes lighting up.

"I wouldn't be quite so melodramatic about it."

"But you are a secret agent?" she insisted.

"If that's what you want to call it," he answered.

"What agency do you work for?"

He stared at her for a long time. "You haven't heard of us. Very few people have."

"And no one will hear about it from me."

Slowly he nodded. "I believe you, Jessica. I know I can trust you." He took a deep breath. "I work for an agency called SPEAR. We've been in existence for a long time. Abraham Lincoln started SPEAR during the Civil War, and we've been around ever since.

We handle problems that are too delicate to give to the more publicity-hungry agencies. We operate in the background, and very few people know we exist.''

''Is Devane an agent, too?''

''Yeah, and the other men who've worked with us.''

''And who is Simon?''

He hesitated for a moment, and she could see that he wanted to brush her off. But finally he nodded. ''You deserve to know that, too. We believe Simon used to be one of us. But he's been trying to destroy the agency for the past year. We've been trying to catch him for a long time.''

Her heart contracted painfully in her chest. Marcus trusted her with information that few other people knew. ''Why did he try to kidnap me?''

''He needs money very badly. We've managed to foil his schemes lately, and he's running out of cash. He probably figured your father would pay a lot, with no questions asked, to get you back.''

''He was right. My father would have paid anything. But how did he decide to kidnap me?''

Marcus shrugged. ''We're not sure. He's been in this part of the world for a while and he probably heard about your father. I suspect you were his fall-back plan, and he put your kidnapping in motion after his last scheme fell through. We got a tip that he was heading for Cascadilla, although no one knew why. I came here to wait for him.''

''So when I told you that Steve and Tommy talked about Simon, you knew exactly who I meant.''

He nodded, and his gaze never flinched. ''I couldn't tell you the truth, Jessica. I had no idea who you were. I knew nothing about you or your possible connections to Simon. But as soon as I knew Simon was behind the scheme, I got SPEAR involved.''

''I understand,'' she said softly, and caught a look of surprise in Marcus's eyes. ''I'm not angry at you for not telling me the truth. But you might have told me sooner.''

''I should have.'' She saw a whisper of regret in his eyes. ''But I'm not used to trusting anyone. It's a hard habit to break.''

''Not many people have given you reason to trust them,'' she murmured. ''And I suspect that includes women you've known.''

He looked away. ''I don't get involved with women. Asking them to share this life isn't fair.''

She wanted to protest, to tell him that wasn't true, but instead she studied him for a moment. ''What happened?'' she finally asked.

He turned his face to hers, surprised. ''What do you mean?''

''It's obvious something happened.''

He shrugged, but his eyes got hard. ''It was a long time ago. And it doesn't matter anymore.''

''I think it does matter.'' Clearly it had left scars.

Marcus hesitated, running his hand through his blond hair. Then he sighed.

''Her name was Heather,'' he said, his mouth tightening. ''I fancied myself in love with her. But she didn't want to marry a spy. She came from money and she wanted me to quit my job and find one that was more...socially acceptable, more mainstream.'' He looked away. ''She made me choose, and I chose my job.''

''Foolish woman,'' Jessica murmured.

''Practical,'' he corrected. ''She knew I wouldn't

be around very much. She knew my job was dangerous. She was just being pragmatic.''

"You're not practical and pragmatic about a man you love,'' she said hotly.

"It really doesn't matter,'' he said again. "It was a long time ago.''

But it did matter. No wonder he was so reluctant to get involved. No wonder he tried so hard to keep her at a distance.

But she wasn't going to let him brush her aside, she told herself fiercely. She wasn't going to let him throw away what they had together.

He glanced at her, then stood to look out the window. "It's going to be light soon,'' he said without looking at her. "As soon as the sun is up, I'll take you back to your parents' island.''

Chapter 17

Her throat constricted, and her heart lurched in her chest. "I'm not ready to go home."

"I'm sure your parents are anxious to see you." He spoke without turning.

"And I want to reassure them. But I'm not ready to say goodbye to you." She knew that if he left, she would never see him again.

"We've said all there is to say, Jessica. I've told you all along that you deserve someone far better than me. You deserve someone as young, as fresh and as alive as you. You deserve to spend your life with someone who can give you everything I can't."

"And what would that be?"

He spun toward her, and she saw the pain on his face. "You got a taste of my world these last few weeks, and don't tell me you liked it. My world is betrayal, ugliness and death. I can't tar you with that brush."

"Marcus, I've only known you for three weeks," she said, her voice level. "But we met under pretty unusual circumstances, and I thought I had learned a lot about you. I've seen you under a lot of stress. I've see you in dangerous situations. But I've never see you do anything cowardly."

She leaned over the table and fixed her gaze on his eyes. "If you take me back to my parents' and run away, you're a coward."

His eyes hardened, and she thought for a moment that she had pushed him too far. But then he shook his head and sat back. "That was very good, but I'm not falling for it. After everything you've seen the past few weeks, and especially after what happened here tonight, you can't tell me that you want to be part of this world." His face looked like it had been carved from granite. "I saw your face tonight. You were horrified."

"Of course I was horrified," she said impatiently. "A man was killed here tonight. But if you hadn't killed him, he would have killed both of us. I understand that, and it has nothing to do with you and me."

"It has everything to do with you and me," he said grimly. "That's what I do for a living."

"I know that," she said gently. "And I'm not saying I wouldn't worry about you. Of course I'll worry. But I would worry if you were a city cop. I'd worry if you worked in a factory." She leaned back but didn't take her gaze off his face, and her mouth curled into a smile. "I'd worry if you dived into the ocean for a living."

He scowled, but she thought she saw a spark of hope in the back of his eyes. "We're not talking about what you do for a living."

"Why not? My work is dangerous, too."

"That's different."

"Different how?"

He scowled again. "It just is. Don't try to confuse the issue here, Jessica."

"And what exactly is the issue?" she asked.

"The issue is whether I'm what you need in your life. And the answer is no."

"You're wrong, Marcus. You're exactly what I need. And I'll prove it to you."

He crossed his arms. "I'd like to see you try."

"I'm sure you would." She stood and took his hand, drawing him to his feet. He stared at her, his eyes uncertain and wary. But the hope she'd seen earlier was more than a spark now. It flickered brightly in the blue depths of his eyes.

Wrapping her arms around his neck, she pressed herself against him and pulled his mouth to hers. He stood rigidly for a moment, then he groaned and gathered her close.

The scared girl who had awakened in his bed three weeks earlier had disappeared completely, she realized. In her place was a woman who knew what she wanted and was willing to fight for it. She and Marcus belonged together. They fit together perfectly, in every aspect of their lives. And she was willing to risk herself, risk humiliation, to make it happen.

"I want you, Marcus," she said. "Will you make love to me?"

He opened his eyes and stared at her. She saw passion and need glittering in his eyes. And something more, something that squeezed her heart and sent joy rocketing through her veins.

"When you touch me, I can't think of anything

else,'' he muttered, weaving his hands through her hair. "I need you more than I need my next breath."

Wordlessly she kissed him again as he traced his hands over her face. His hands were gentle, caressing her with a touch as light as a kiss. It almost felt like he was memorizing her. Then he groaned and deepened the kiss, and she tasted his desperation and his need.

His hands trembled as they raced over her, and a fire leaped to life in her belly. When she began fumbling with the buttons on his shirt, he picked her up and carried her into the bedroom.

She wanted to seduce him, but suddenly their roles were reversed. As his fingers loosened her clothes, his mouth trailed kisses behind them, tasting her everywhere. When she pulled at his shirt, needing to feel his body against hers, he trapped both her hands in one of his and held her still. And he continued to kiss her, his mouth tasting and suckling until she writhed on the bed beneath him.

"I need you, Marcus. I need to touch you."

He lifted his head, his eyes bright with desire. "You'll get your turn," he murmured. "You have to learn a little patience, Jessica."

"Maybe you can teach me," she said, pulling her hands free from his and rolling him over. She straddled him, then lightly held his wrists. "It's my turn now."

He twined his fingers with hers and smiled. "That's only fair, I suppose."

"You suppose right." Still holding his hands, she bent to kiss him. When she moved lower and swirled her tongue around his nipple, he tensed beneath her. She smiled against his skin, loving the male taste of him, the hardness of his muscles, the way he trembled when she touched him.

Then she slid lower, and he groaned, his hands tightening on hers.

"Jessica," he panted. "Oh, Jess."

Desire grew inside her, throbbing and insistent. Marcus suddenly lifted her and rolled her over, then joined himself to her. She opened her eyes to see him staring at her. Tenderness filled his eyes, and she had never seen him more open, more vulnerable. "I want everything to be perfect for you," he whispered.

She reached for him, and he covered her mouth with his. And when he moved inside her, more than their bodies were joined. Her heart belonged to him, forever.

They lay together for a long time, holding each other, their hands twined together. Finally she said, "Did you mean it?"

"Mean what?"

"When you said you wanted everything to be perfect for me."

He shifted so that she was pressed tighter against his shoulder. "Of course I meant it. I want everything to be perfect for you, always."

"Then you know that you're perfect for me. You're the only one, Marcus."

His arms tightened around her, but he couldn't say a word.

"I love you," she said. "I always will."

"You can't love me," he said, but his heart ached to believe her.

"Why not? Don't you love me?"

Slowly he pulled away from her. He knew exactly how much courage it had taken for her to say that to him. And he was ashamed of himself for his lack of courage.

He took a deep breath. "Of course I love you. Why do you think I've been so determined to leave you? It's because I love you more than life. I don't want you to throw your life away with me."

She framed his face with her hands. "You're the only man on earth who can make me happy, Marcus. We belong together. I love you, and I'm not going to let you go." She grinned at him. "And I'd like to see you try and make me."

"What kind of miracle are you?" he whispered. "You know you're everything I want. I just can't believe you want me, too."

Her smile faded. "More than anything in the world," she said, her voice shaking. "Please don't leave me, Marcus."

He reached out and cupped her cheek in his hand. "I don't think I could if my life depended on it." He stared at her for a moment, wonder filling his heart. Then he swept her into his arms. "I'll spend the rest of my life trying to make you happy."

"You already have," she said.

"I'm going to call my boss and quit," he said, ignoring the pang in his chest. "I don't want to spend my life separated from you."

She leaned back and searched his face. "You don't have to do that," she said quietly. "I know how much you love your job."

"But I love you more." He looked at her, amazed that it was the truth. "I never imagined I would say that to a woman. But it's true. My job isn't the most important thing in my life anymore. You are."

"But that doesn't mean you have to quit." She

traced her hand over his jaw, then touched his lips. "You love your job, and you're good at it. So why would you quit?"

"Because I might have to be gone from you for months at a time. I don't think I could bear that."

"Promise me you won't make a decision until you catch Simon," she said. "I know how important that is."

Before he could answer, the telephone rang. He looked at her, and she nodded, knowing exactly what he asked. "Of course you have to answer it."

He was back in moments, slipping into the bed next to her. "What happened?" he said into the cell phone, listening to Russell Devane.

"Are you sure?" he asked after a long time. Then he said, "All right. It sounds like it might work. But be careful," he added softly. "I'll catch up with you."

"What is it?" she asked when he closed the phone.

"That was Russell Devane. They got the phone records and found the address where Simon was staying. But by the time they got there, he was gone. They managed to trace him to the airport, but his plane had just taken off. For Australia."

"What is he going to do in Australia?" she asked.

"We'll find out. Devane is going to take on Steve Trace's identity and follow Simon to Australia. Simon never saw Trace and doesn't know he's dead. Devane might be able to get close to him and capture him." He longed to be there, but he didn't want to leave Jessica.

"You can't quit now," she said gently. "SPEAR needs you. You have to go."

"All right." He pulled her close and kissed her

again, the excitement of the chase blending with regret at leaving her. "But I'll be back as soon as I can."

"I know." She curled her arms around him and leaned into him. "I'll miss you horribly, but I'm going to be busy, too. I have to finish my dissertation and get my Ph.D." She smiled into his throat. "And just think how much fun our reunions are going to be."

"I won't be a field agent forever," he said. "I'm not getting any younger. What are you going to do with me when I'm a desk jockey and around all the time?"

"I have plans for you." She reached up and kissed him. "I think you might enjoy them. And I'm planning on keeping you very busy." She leaned back and grinned. "Someone is going to have to help me with all those children we're going to have."

His heart swelled in his chest until he felt like it would burst. Jessica was everything he'd ever wanted in his life and everything he'd been afraid he'd never find. "It sounds like you have me backed into a corner," he said, his voice husky.

"I hope so. I don't plan on giving you any choice here."

As if he would want one. "Then I guess we'll have to get married." He took her hand and kissed her knuckles. "Will you marry me, Jessica?"

Her eyes glittered with tears. "Yes, Marcus," she whispered. "There's nothing I want more."

As he bent his head to kiss her, dawn eased its way into the room, bathing them both in the golden light of a new day. His heart expanded with joy until he thought it would burst. He'd been waiting all his life for Jessica. He just hadn't known it. She was all the dreams he hadn't dared to dream come to life.

She leaned away from him and smiled, as if she knew what he was thinking. "I love you, Marcus. You've made all my dreams come true."

She'd been able to read his mind from the very beginning. "I love you, too, Jessica. Forever."

*   *   *   *   *

Next month, look for

THE ENEMY'S DAUGHTER

by Linda Turner
as Intimate Moments' exciting

A YEAR OF LOVING DANGEROUSLY

series continues.
Turn the page for a sneak preview...

Chapter 1

Staring out at the barren desert that was the Australian Outback, Russell Devane had, before he'd accepted this particular mission, thought he was a man who could take in stride whatever nature threw at him. After all, his job as an operative for the secret organization, SPEAR, had taken him to the farthest reaches of the globe. He'd withstood the bone numbing cold of the Arctic and the throat parching heat of the Sahara, all without complaint. But he could already see that nothing in his past had really prepared him for the Outback. It was the tail end of summer— Fall was just days away—but the temperature had to be a hundred and twenty degrees in the shade. And it wasn't even noon yet!

Just thinking about working in that kind of heat all day long made him sweat, but he grimly resolved to get used to it. He had to. In a few minutes, he would be arriving at the headquarters of the Pear Tree Cattle

Station, where he would assume the identity of Steve Trace, the station's newest cowboy and an associate of Art Meldrum, the owner of the place.

To the rest of the world, Art was an absentee landlord who left the running of the huge ranch in the hands of his daughter, Lise, most of the time. Only Russell—and his fellow SPEAR operatives—knew that Art was actually an alias for Simon, the traitor who'd spent the last eight months trying his damnedest to destroy not only Jonah, the head of SPEAR, but the agency itself. And he was slippery as an eel. Time and again, just when SPEAR operatives were sure they had him in their grasp, he'd managed to slip away.

Not this time, Russell promised himself, his gray eyes steely as he thought of how Simon had evaded capture just days ago on the Caribbean island of Cascadilla. The bastard had, in fact, never even put in an appearance on the island. Thanks to the real Steve Trace, a kidnapper and thug who'd been hired sight unseen by Simon, he'd been warned he was walking into a trap if he came to Cascadilla. So he'd run home to the Outback, where he could lie low in the bush, and he'd never known that Steve Trace had died soon after he'd gotten word to him he was in danger.

SPEAR had made sure that no one knew of Trace's death, making it easy for Russell to step right into his life. Pretending to be Trace, he'd called Simon and given him a sob story about needing a job. Not suspecting a thing, Simon had told him to come to the station, which was just what Russell had figured would happen. After all, Simon had narrowly escaped capture thanks to the quick thinking of Trace. The least he owed him was a job.

So here he was two days later, right in Simon's own backyard, and so damn close to the bastard he swore he could smell him. And Simon didn't have a clue what kind of trouble was coming his way. Russell hoped he enjoyed his freedom because it was just about to come to an end.

The station headquarters came into view then, just a dot on the horizon that grew steadily larger with every passing mile. Long moments later, the mailman Russell had hitched a ride with just outside of Roo Springs pulled up before the main house in a swirl of dust. "Here you are, mate," he said, frowning at the house. "The place looks deserted."

Russell had to agree. Set in the middle of the barren plain without so much as a single tree to offer shade, the large, two-story frame house appeared empty. There were no cars in sight and nothing moved but the dust stirred up by the wind.

Shooting him a frown, the mailman arched a dark brow at him. "You sure you're expected? Lise usually sticks close to the house when company's coming. She doesn't get many visitors way out here in the bush."

If anyone would know Lise's schedule, Russell figured it would be the mailman. Roo Springs was the closest town to the station—if you could call a wide spot in the road with fifty inhabitants a town—and there was only one mailman to deliver the mail. There was probably little that went on within a two hundred mile radius that the older man didn't know about.

"I didn't know exactly when I would be arriving," Russell replied, which was the truth. "I'll just unload my stuff and wait on the front porch until she gets back."

The postman, who was as thin and scrawny as the scraggly bushes planted in the dust in the yard, looked anything but convinced. "I don't know, mate. It's a warm day, and you being a Yank and all, you should be inside out of the heat. Let me see if I can raise somebody." And with no more warning than that, he laid on the horn.

Wincing, Russell swore. Damn idiot! He'd hoped he'd have a chance to look around the place without being observed, but then again, he hadn't expected to arrive with horns blaring like the leader of a damn parade either! This was great. Just great!

Muttering under his breath, he started to tell the old man to lay off, but just then, his eyes fell on the corral next to the barn on the far side of the house. His heart stopped dead in his chest at the sight of a woman nearly under the hooves of what appeared to be a wild mustang rearing on its hind legs. Frightened by the horn, its eyes wide, the horse looked ready to stomp her into the ground.

Later, Russell never remembered moving. One second, he was all set to chew out the mailman and the next, he was out of the vehicle and charging across the compound at a dead run toward the corral.

If someone had asked him then what she looked like, he couldn't have said. All he saw was a woman in trouble. Hopping the fence, he swept her up into his arms like she weighed no more than a feather and set her out of harm's way on the other side of the corral fence.

Only then did he take a good look at her. She was a big girl, 5'11" if she was an inch, with a cloud of auburn hair that fell nearly to her waist and skin that was rose-petal soft under his hands. Tanned from working outside, her eyes as blue as the sky, she was trim and fit and had the kind of fresh-faced, subtle beauty that a lot of men often overlooked. Not Russell. In the stark barrenness of the Outback, she was an unexpected treasure...

Silhouette®

INTIMATE MOMENTS™

presents a riveting 12-book continuity series:

A Year of loving dangerously

Where passion rules and nothing is what it seems...

When dishonor threatens a top-secret agency, the brave
men and women of SPEAR are prepared to risk it all as they
put their lives—and their hearts—on the line.

Available March 2001:

THE ENEMY'S DAUGHTER
by Linda Turner

When undercover SPEAR agent Russell Devane arrived at the
Pear Tree cattle station deep in the Australian outback, he had every
intention of getting close to the enemy's daughter. But all the rules
changed when Russell found himself fighting a forbidden attraction
to the breathtakingly beautiful Lise. Would he be able to capture
an evil traitor without forfeiting the love of a lifetime?

*Available only from Silhouette Intimate Moments
at your favorite retail outlet.*

Silhouette®
Where love comes alive™

Visit Silhouette at www.eHarlequin.com   SIMAYOLD10

where love comes alive—online...

eHARLEQUIN.com

shop eHarlequin

♥ Find all the new Silhouette releases at everyday great discounts.

♥ Try before you buy! Read an excerpt from the latest Silhouette novels.

♥ Write an online review and share your thoughts with others.

reading room

♥ Read our Internet exclusive daily and weekly online serials, or vote in our interactive novel.

♥ Talk to other readers about your favorite novels in our Reading Groups.

♥ Take our Choose-a-Book quiz to find the series that matches you!

authors' alcove

♥ Find out interesting tidbits and details about your favorite authors' lives, interests and writing habits.

♥ Ever dreamed of being an author? Enter our Writing Round Robin. The Winning Chapter will be published online! Or review our writing guidelines for submitting your novel.

a Year of Loving dangerously

If you missed the first 7 riveting,
romantic Intimate Moments stories
from *A Year of Loving Dangerously*,
here's a chance to order your copies today!

#1016	**MISSION: IRRESISTIBLE** by Sharon Sala	$4.50 U.S.☐ $5.25 CAN.☐
#1022	**UNDERCOVER BRIDE** by Kylie Brant	$4.50 U.S.☐ $5.25 CAN.☐
#1028	**NIGHT OF NO RETURN** by Eileen Wilks	$4.50 U.S.☐ $5.25 CAN.☐
#1034	**HER SECRET WEAPON** by Beverly Barton	$4.50 U.S.☐ $5.25 CAN.☐
#1040	**HERO AT LARGE** by Robyn Amos	$4.50 U.S.☐ $5.25 CAN.☐
#1046	**STRANGERS WHEN WE MARRIED**	
	by Carla Cassidy	$4.50 U.S.☐ $5.25 CAN.☐
#1052	**THE SPY WHO LOVED HIM**	
	by Merline Lovelace	$4.50 U.S.☐ $5.25 CAN.☐

(limited quantities available)

TOTAL AMOUNT	$ _____
POSTAGE & HANDLING	
($1.00 each book, 50¢ each additional book)	$ _____
APPLICABLE TAXES*	$ _____
TOTAL PAYABLE	$ _____
(check or money order—please do not send cash)	

To order, send the completed form, along with a check or money order for the total
above, payable to **A YEAR OF LOVING DANGEROUSLY** to: **In the U.S.:** 3010 Walden
Avenue, P.O. Box 9077, Buffalo, NY 14269-9077; **In Canada:** P.O. Box 636, Fort Erie,
Ontario L2A 5X3.

Name: _____

Address: _____ City: _____

State/Prov.: _____ Zip/Postal Code: _____

Account # (if applicable): _____ 075 CSAS

*New York residents remit applicable sales taxes.
Canadian residents remit applicable
GST and provincial taxes.

Silhouette®

Visit Silhouette at www.eHarlequin.com   AYOLD-BL7